MR AND MRS MCGREGOR'S HONEYMOON ON THE ISLAND OF SANTORINI, GREECE

Michael Nwaduba

Grosvenor House
Publishing Limited

The right of Michael Nwaduba to be identified as the author of this
work has been asserted in accordance with Section 78
of the Copyright, Designs and Patents Act 1988

The book cover picture is copyright to Michael Nwaduba

This book is published by
Grosvenor House Publishing Ltd
Link House
140 The Broadway, Tolworth, Surrey, KT6 7HT.
www.grosvenorhousepublishing.co.uk

NOTE:

This book is a work of fiction and some of the characters are fictitious as well
as some places mentioned. If any fictitious character resembles anyone living,
it's simply a coincidence, and the author is truly sorry for that.

Any use of the information in this book is entirely at the reader's discretion
and risk. The author or publisher cannot be held liable for any loss, claim, or
damage arising out of the use or misuse of the suggestions made in this book.

Due to the dynamic nature of the internet, website addresses or links used in
this book may have changed since publication and may no longer be valid.
Hence, the author and publisher hereby disclaim any responsibility for them.

A CIP record for this book
is available from the British Library

Paperback ISBN 978-1-83615-427-3
eBook ISBN 978-1-83615-428-0

CONTENTS

CHAPTER ONE

DAY 1 – SUNDAY
THE ISLAND OF SANTORINI, GREECE

Shaun McGregor and Mary Jenkins just got married on Christmas Day in London, England. They were joined together by Bishop John Barnes at the Shekinah Pentecostal Church. It was a glorious wedding ceremony attended by many family members, and friends. This wonderful blessed couple, Mr and Mrs McGregor, are now ready to commence their two-week honeymoon on the Island of Santorini, Greece.

Shaun kept the location of the honeymoon as a secret from his wife until after the wedding. He made all the necessary visa, hotel, and tour booking preparations ready without getting her involved. He wants to give her a fantastic honeymoon surprise. As a millionaire, he did all that without any financial hassle, and he did it with joy to please his amazing beautiful wife.

After the wedding, and the reception activities, they walked down to their special luxury *Rolls-Royce Limousine Charlotte* car.

The Chauffeur said to them, "Congratulations Mr and Mrs McGregor."

And they answered, "Thank you."

The Chauffeur introduced himself and said, "My name is Daniel King. I came from the Goldstar Car

Company." He opened the car doors for them, and as they all sat down, he said, "Please make yourselves comfortable and relax with the wine, music, and sweets," and he drove off, heading to Gatwick Airport.

Mary turned to her husband, and with a beaming warm smile on her beautiful face, and with her hand on his shoulder, she started a conversation and asked him with a gentle, loving tone, "Honey, where are we having the honeymoon?"

He finally told her as he answered, "On the Island of Santorini, Greece."

She screamed out aloud, "Whao! I love it. This is absolutely fantastic."

Shaun said, "That's good. I'm glad you love our honeymoon destination," and he asked, "So, why do you love it?"

And she replied, "Anything my husband likes, I like too," and she laughed as she held Shaun's hand. That's the true spirit of followership in a marriage. As a wife, and help meet for your husband, you try your very best to align with his goals, and vision as the head and leader. This will greatly enhance peace and progress in the marriage. This is one of the things Mary learnt in the marriage counselling sessions.

Mary continued and said, "This trip will give me the opportunity to learn more about Greek culture and traditions." She carried on and said, "Honey, you know the New Testament of the Bible was written originally in Greek. This will be a very good opportunity for us to learn more about the Greek language, ancient history, archaeology, and mythology. I hope we will visit the museum."

He replied, "Yes, you are right. It's part of the reason why I chose Greece, and also determined to make it a surprise for you."

Mary asked again, "What else made you choose the Island of Santorini, Greece?"

Shaun cleared his throat and continued, "Actually, some years ago, I had a business meeting with an oil magnate billionaire business associate on the Island of Santorini. I had a huge successful business negotiation with him that tremendously upgraded my company to an unbelievable next level. Since then, I fell in love with the Island of Santorini. I was captivated by the beauty, serenity, and glamour I experienced on the Island, and I thought this honeymoon would be a perfect opportunity to do a repeat visit with my lovely wife." He paused while they looked at each other with lovely smiles radiating on their faces.

Shaun continued and said, "The Island of Santorini is a very popular honeymoon destination for couples. The wealthy and famous, business tycoons, celebrities, and even Hollywood stars also visit Santorini on holidays. Hollywood has produced some marvellous movies on the Island of Santorini, Greece. They have very good tourist attractions, the beautiful sea, rocks, and sunny views, hotels, good food, and wines in Santorini and other neighbouring Greece Islands which includes Anafi, Folegandros, Milos, Ios, Paros, Naxos, and Mykonos."[1]

Mary replied, "You are the best husband in the world. Thank you for taking me to such a beautiful Island. I'm already over the moon as we start this honeymoon journey. I love you darling."

Shaun, with a feeling of elation, and with a smile on his face replied, "I love you too sweetheart," and he gave her a kiss. And she said, "Thank you darling."

The Chauffeur arrives at the Gatwick Airport, and the couple alight and say goodbye to him, and they make their way straight to the departure section to check in. They are travelling on an Airbus A320 Flight N0. 5555 in the first class section, specially reserved for them as a newlywed couple.

As soon as they got on board the airplane, they got into the first class section, and she saw the decoration on the window side of the airplane with the inscription, "Congratulations, Mr & Mrs McGregor" and two balloons on each end. She said, "Whao! This is absolutely beautiful darling. I love the decoration with our name displayed."

Mr & Mrs McGregor settled down and fastened their seat belts as they took off to the Island of Santorini, Greece. They carried on with their conversation regarding the success of their marriage considering the huge turnout at the ceremony. They are grateful to God. They are also grateful for the many wedding gifts they received. They were now served food and drinks by beautiful flight attendants, and they enjoyed the first class service. London to Santorini is about a 4-hour flight. The pilot announced, "Ladies and gentlemen, we are now approaching Santorini Airport, Greece. Please fasten your seat belts for safety as we begin to descend. Thank you." They both said, "So quick. We are almost there. Thank you, Lord Jesus."

As soon as they landed, they both said, "Thank you, Jesus." They made their way towards the exit and to the Immigration office. As they moved on, she said, "This Santorini Airport is beautiful." They got to the Immigration office, and met the officer. He said to them, "My name is Aristotle. I hope you had a nice flight? They both answered, "Yes."

Aristotle asked for their passports, and as he checked them, he asked, "How long are you going to be with us in Greece? They said, "Two weeks." He stamped their passports and said, "Enjoy your honeymoon."

They replied, "Efcharisto." This means "Thank you," in Greek.

Aristotle answered and said, "Parakalo," which means "You are welcome." They waved goodbye to him as they had now been cleared and allowed to enter Santorini, Greece.

Shaun and Mary had earlier gone onto the internet to check out simple greetings and words in Greek, and they were eager to try some out at the slightest opportunity.

When they came out of the arrival section, they met Constantine, the Chauffeur arranged by Perfecto 5-star hotel to pick them up. Constantine was waving a little placard with their name written on it, "Mr & Mrs McGregor." They saw him, met him and with a beaming smile on his handsome face, he had a firm handshake with Shaun, and he said in Greek language, "Ονομάζομαι Κωνσταντίνος και είμαι από το ξενοδοχείο 5 αστέρων Perfecto." This means, "My name is Constantine, and I am from Perfecto 5-star hotel."

Shaun replied in Greek, "Το όνομά μου είναι Shaun και αυτή είναι η σύζυγός μου Mary." Meaning "My name is Shaun and this is my wife Mary."

Constantine replied, "Parakalo."

They all got into the luxury *Rolls-Royce Phantom 8* car and Constantine drove off heading for the Perfecto 5-star hotel on the seaside in Fira, the capital town of the Island of Santorini. Athens is the capital of Greece. They also have other good hotels in Fira, Island of Santorini, Greece like Katikies Garden Hotel, You and Me Suites, Athina Luxury Suites, Iriana Suites, Golden Grey Goose, and Cosmopolitan Suites.[2]

As they arrived at the Perfecto 5-star hotel, they alighted from the car and went with their luggage to the reception for registration. Perfecto is an exclusive luxury 5-star hotel for Christian couples on their honeymoon, holidays, Men and Women of God, Christian organization groups who come for prayer retreats and revival, bourgeois, tycoons, and celebrities who desire a serene godly atmosphere. Shaun specially chose it as a surprise for her. They both have positive surprises for each other that will take them over the moon in this once-in-a-lifetime honeymoon.

At the reception, they met a beautiful young Greek girl. She introduced herself to them as Sophia and attended to them. She asked in Greek, "Πώς σε λένε?" meaning, "What is your name?" Shaun replied, "Mr and Mrs McGregor." She quickly pulled up their files on the computer, asked for their passports for identification, while asking some other questions, completed their details and declared their registration complete, and gave them their suite details and keys.

It's Christmas Day, and while they were still at the reception, they played Greek Christmas carol songs. As the songs played, the vibrant newlywed pair began to enjoy the songs, held hands, and all eyes at the reception were fastened on them, but they seemed not to notice because they were in their own world of honeymoon.

They proceeded to their lavishly furnished suite. Everything in this suite is massive, classy, and unique. The fantastic chandelier ceiling lights, decorations and artwork displayed on the walls caught her attention, and then the amenities. She stood still and started looking at each of the following beautiful canvas-made pictures displayed on the wall: Jesus picture; Mary and Jesus in the manger; Jesus' last supper with the disciples; canvas pictures showing the seaside, sky, ship, rocks, mountains, and forest trees; traditional, cultural, native, Greek houses, clothes, wines, food etc. were on display both on the wall as pictures, pottery vessels, and on wood carvings. Absolutely beautiful.

They both went from the sitting room to the bedroom and saw the wardrobes, king-size bed, upholstery chairs, lights, air conditioner, mirror, etc. They entered the bathroom and saw the massive Jacuzzi, shower, toilet, mirror, white robes and towels, beautiful wall decorations and tiles. Everything is white, very clean, and well arranged.

They got back to the balcony and had a good view of the exterior part of the Island of Santorini from the Perfecto hotel. With a great feeling of satisfaction and marvel, she said, "It's very hard for me to put into words the magnificence and beauty of this palace. I call it a palace because I am amazed and dazzled by what I have seen. You must have spent a fortune on this. Thank you very much darling. Much appreciated. My God will richly reward you for all your care and love in

Jesus' name." He said, "Amen! You are welcome darling."

Mary got out her anointing oil and began to anoint the hotel suite to banish every evil spirit from the suite because of the high traffic of all manner of people that use the hotel suite. She anointed the bed, wardrobe, front door, windows, chairs, tables, etc. As she did this, she spoke in tongues, casting out every evil spirit and invoking the blood of Jesus on the entire apartment suite. Evil spirits are real. In Mark 5, Jesus cast out evil spirits from a mad man, and they entered into swine. Luke 22:3 tells us that Satan entered Judas. So Satan enters people. When she finished doing the anointing, Shaun said, "Thanks for doing the anointing darling. Now we can stay in this Suite with the consciousness that the devil cannot mess about or harass us in Jesus' name." She said, "Amen! You are welcome honey."

She started unpacking their clothes and shoes from their suitcases and arranging them in the wardrobe. After she finished doing that, she got into the bathroom and called out to Shawn to join her, but he did not come to the bathroom. She brushed her teeth and tongue thoroughly in order to enhance fresh breath, good dental care, and kisses.

Mary undressed herself and came out of the bathroom completely naked, exposing her very attractive breasts, nipples, and vulva pubic hair as she went into the sitting room. Absolute beauty from head to toe. No blemish! No rashes, pimples, scars or tattoos. Mary is fully aware of what the Bible says about tattoos in:

Leviticus 19:28 (New Living Translation – (NLT) says, "Do not cut your bodies for the dead, and <u>do not</u>

*mark your skin with tattoos. I am the L*ORD.*"* (Underline mine)

Mary honors and reveres God. Therefore, she has no tattoos. The Bible also makes it clear in 1 Corinthians 3:16-17, and 6:19, that our body is the temple of the Holy Spirit, and anyone who defiles this temple, God will destroy. Part of the danger of anyone having tattoos all over their face and body is that they may not be able to get certain jobs, marry certain people, and tattoos are irreversible. As a Christian, focus on reading your Bible and meditation, to acquire more knowledge and wisdom which will build you up, and increase your value inwardly, rather than drawing tattoos on your body externally which are virtually of no value, and God is also against it. Keep your body clean for your spouse. You are already fearfully and wonderfully made by God. See Psalm 139:14. Mary is a complete embodiment of natural beauty.

Mary called out Shaun for the second time, thinking he would be moved to see her nudity, but he answered and said, "Please carry on darling. When you finish, I will come and freshen up."

She replied, "What do you mean? I don't understand. Let's have a shower together."

Shaun said again, "Please carry on darling. I will do mine when you finish." At this point, she became a bit concerned and suspicious considering Shaun's tone and body language. She quickly had her shower alone and came out and told him she has finished.

Shaun got into the bathroom and washed his teeth and tongue thoroughly. He had his shower and also put on his pajamas, and a bit of his *Hugo Boss* perfume.

While he did that, Mary robbed her cream, put on her beautiful nightgown, and her *Chanel Chance Eau de parfum* spray. She dressed her hair properly, and she is now ready for action.

Once a couple is legally married, that gives them full license to have sex. Sex is a very important aspect of a couple's marriage. Apart from the purpose of procreation, sex refreshes. Have sex often, and if you've got the strength, do it daily. Whenever the word 'sex' is mentioned, some Christians frown at it as if it's a taboo to do so, and they do so perhaps out of pretext or ignorance.

Of what use is a honeymoon without talking about sex or having sex? If you don't want to talk about sex or have sex on a honeymoon, that's already an indication and proof that you are probably in the wrong marriage, or you are a hypocrite, or a deceiver, because sexual intercourse is a MUST to achieve deeper intimacy on a marriage honeymoon. The Bible says in Genesis 1:28, "And God blessed them, and God said unto them, Be fruitful, and multiply, and replenish the earth, and subdue it:…" Can a couple multiply without sex?

Many marriages are no longer exciting, and some others are as good as dead because romance, love, and constant sex have been excluded. Rekindle the fire in your marriage by engaging in serious romance, love, and sex. God created sex for married couples to enjoy. Therefore, enjoy it.

Mary has been looking forward to having sex with her husband, especially on their wedding day, and the first day of their honeymoon, but she's wondering why

Shaun is not responding excitedly to have a shower with her as a newlywed couple who have been in a courtship for one year without sex.

Mary went to her husband Shaun in the sitting room and sat beside him on the sofa, and asked, "Honey, are you ok? Why did you not join me for a shower?"

He replied, "Well, I was tired, and I didn't feel like it."

She said, "Really?" She held her husband and wrapped her hands around him, and smiled and said, "I love you honey."

And Shaun replied, "I love you too," and they both started caressing and kissing. As they did that, Mary moved her hand down to Shaun's penis and noticed that it was very small, and she could barely grab it properly. What! She was baffled and deflated, but tried not to show it as she pulled his pajamas down for her to see the penis properly. Behold, it is very small indeed even with full erection.

They carried on cuddling and kissing, to the point when they went into the bedroom and Mary lay on the bed in the *Missionary-style sex position*, and he penetrated her with his small penis and made a few sluggish jerks and ejaculated sperm into her. She could hardly feel the penis and did not enjoy the sex at all, but knew he ejaculated and deposited sperm into her. A very disappointing sex session from a big man like Shaun. For her, this is child's play because it is far below her expectations on this first honeymoon sex encounter. This was when Mary now realized why Shaun did not join her to shower together, because he did not want her to see his small penis.

Immediately after this first round of unexpected and unimpressive sex, the devil swung into action and started bombarding Mary.

MR DEVIL: Can you see why it is very important to have sex before marriage? If you had had sex with Shaun before marriage, you would have known he had a tiny penis and got rid of him.

MARY MCGREGOR: Mary being a woman of faith retorted, "Get thee behind me Satan, it's none of your business. My Bible tells me in:

1 Corinthians 6:18-20

> [18] *Flee fornication. Every sin that a man doeth is without the body; but he that committeth fornication sinneth against his own body.*

> [19] *What? know ye not that your body is the temple of the Holy Ghost which is in you, which ye have of God, and ye are not your own?*

> [20] *For ye are bought with a price: therefore glorify God in your body, and in your spirit, which are God's."*

MR DEVIL: Can you see that size matters when it comes to penis and sex enjoyment? Shaun couldn't perform with a tiny penis.

MARY MCGREGOR: Mary declared again to the devil, "*I walk by faith and not by sight.*" - *2 Corinthians 5:7*. Therefore, size does not matter. Mind you, my husband ejaculated sperm into me, and that will get me pregnant to have a baby.

MR DEVIL: Do you mean you will put up with this tiny penis all the days of your life and not enjoy sex? You know that will drag you into cheating and unfaithfulness, as you desire to try out a man with a big penis.

MARY MCGREGOR: No way, Mr Devil. You are a liar. I will never commit adultery with another man, with a small or big penis. I have learnt to be content with whatever I have, as my Bible says in:

Philippians 4:11

> *Not that I speak in respect of want: for I have learned, in whatsoever state I am, therewith to be content.*

After Mary resisted the devil the way our Lord Jesus Christ also confronted and defeated him in the wilderness in Matthew 4, and Luke 4 by declaring the scriptures 3 times, *"It is written."* The devil fled. Like Father, like daughter. The Bible says in:

James 4:7

> *Submit yourselves therefore to God. Resist the devil, and he will flee from you.*

Mary resisted the devil and he fled.

Mary is determined that the way Shaun's strong Scottish accent has gone unnoticeable to her, that's how this small penis issue will also go unnoticeable. That's a spiritual, mature Christian way of thinking and handling matters. Mary is fully aware that marriage can be full of unexpected and unpleasant surprises because couples do turn up with all manner of bags and baggage as a package. Emotional pain, bitterness, unforgiveness etc. inclusive. In a moment, she remembered Alan Brown and Stephen Brown, his 10-year-old son, whom she only got to know about after the death of Alan Brown. Stephen Brown was a surprise to her. What about Donald Bruce? He jilted her when she tried to boss him around and that caused her emotional pain for years. Is anyone really perfect?

Then she considered herself and said, "If not that God healed me, I also had my own tribulations of fibroids and breast cancer, which could have been brought into this marriage." However, as a person of integrity, Mary would have told her fiancé during courtship before marriage. For her, you don't let things you don't have control over worry you unnecessarily. Besides, she knows and believes that all things will always work together for her good because she loves God, and she's called according to His purpose. Mary encouraged and consoled herself.

Mary now got together with her husband in the sitting room, and he started reflecting on this small penis matter and told her his story.

When I was a child, I saw other children's penises, and I realized mine was tiny compared to theirs. From that time, I became ashamed and started hiding my penis.

When I got into high school, and at the age of 15 years, one of my classmates, William Dudley, Alias "Rascal" unexpectedly came into the bathroom one day when I was taking a shower and saw me naked and said, "Boy! Your penis is very small. It's just like the size of a small "okra" slimy fruit. Like that of a 7-year-old boy."

I shouted aloud, "Hey! Shut up and mind your business."

He replied, "Chill men! Have you tried it on any girl? I guarantee you, no girl will stay with you with that tiny thing." And he started mocking me hilariously.

But I was embarrassed and deflated. My ego was punctured, and I didn't know where to hide my face.

The next week, he teased me in the presence of three of my classmates and asked me, "What is it like down there in between your thighs, Shaun? Any improvement in size?" And he giggled. What a rascally embarrassing question and behavior from Rascal! I ignored him, but I was filled with burning rage and anger within. I chose not to react or express it, because if I did, William Dudley would have escalated the matter by telling other students.

Years ago, my first girlfriend, Agnes Jones, denied me sex when she saw my small penis. I tried to persuade her, but she screamed and said, "I will shout for help now and say you want to rape me if you don't leave me." I immediately left her and that ended the relationship.

I have only had sex twice with 2 ladies all my life. Once with each lady. They both refused to have a repeat sex with me because of the small size of my penis.

I remember very vividly my encounter with the last lady, Edna Phillips. I saw her, and I invited her to come and see me, and she told me off in an insulting manner. She said, "You are inviting me to your house to do what? Are you a man? The last time I saw you, were you able to perform? Please get out of my sight." Immediately she said that, I was dumbfounded, and my small penis now shrank completely into my scrotum. Those words tore me apart so much that my eyes were darkened, and I started feeling dizzy, and my feet were like glued to the ground, not able to walk.

I was so shattered by those words to the extent that when I got home, I wept. I felt like my whole world had crumbled. This condition made me not to be keen about approaching ladies anymore for a relationship. I got into a withdrawal mould. Even as a millionaire, I have not had sex with any woman. Instead, I became a born-again Christian and got very serious about my relationship with God.

I approached my doctor for advice, and help with the possibility of penis enlargement in length and girth, but the doctor checked my penis and told me there was nothing he could do to help me. He said it will be risky and dangerous to attempt penis enlargement because it could go wrong and eventually render me impotent.

However, my doctor encouraged me and said that, in terms of performance, impregnating a woman should not be a problem. It's just the sexual satisfaction aspect that may not be fully accomplished. However, once a man is able to penetrate a woman through the vulva, clitoris, and vagina, ejaculate sperm which travels through the cervix, down to the uterus, and an egg released from the female ovary is transported through the fallopian tube to the uterus, positively interacts with the male sperm for fertilization to take place that can lead to a pregnancy.[3-4]

I have always prayed and believed God by faith to enlarge my penis. I also pray that I will find the right woman that will accept me the way I am with my small penis. Today, here I am, married to you. Sorry I didn't tell you during our courtship I had a small penis. I didn't know how to present it to you and what your reaction would be. Please don't leave me darling. You are worth more than the whole world to me. If you leave me, I will be devastated.

Shaun stopped his story and started crying with tears gushing out of his eyes profusely and ceaselessly. It was a heart-breaking moment to behold.

Mary was deeply touched. She was instantly quickened with holy anger in her spirit, and the heavens opened up, and the anointing of the Holy Spirit came upon the woman of God mightily, and she cried out fervently to God, even as King Hezekiah did when the Prophet Isaiah gave him the message from God that he will die.

Mary laid her hand on Shaun's shoulder and cried out aloud to God, saying, "Father God, remember now how I have served you diligently all these years, being obedient to your Word, and eschewing evil and sin. You have been very merciful and forgiving to me, and I say thank you, Lord. You delivered and healed me from fibroids and breast cancer. I prayed for Dominic Lloyds, my former Oxford University colleague who I met at the hospital, and he told me he was inflicted with voodoo by a Caribbean woman and had a continuous erection problem, you healed him instantly and his penis became normal. This is clear evidence that enlarging a small penis to a normal average size is not a hard thing for you to do, because with God all things are possible, including penis enlargement. Lord Jesus, this is your son, my husband, whom you have given to me. Most High God, I ask that you touch his penis right now and enlarge it to be of average normal size for a man in Jesus' name."

She began to speak in tongues so intensely, and suddenly, Shaun screamed out aloud, saying, "Honey, my penis is enlarging." He continued, "This is a miracle, oh! My penis is enlarged and normal."

She stopped praying and said, "Let me see it." She saw the big normally erected penis, and she jumped up for joy, and her head almost touched the ceiling. They both started praising God and dancing. Today was their wedding day and the first day of their honeymoon. What a remarkable day to experience this awesome miracle. Praise God! Hallelujah!

Immediately, Mr & Mrs McGregor got into action to experience the enlarged penis. Mary, out of excitement, grabbed her husband's penis and started licking and sucking it like a lollipop, as in a fellatio with great satisfaction, while Shaun was responding with sighs of enjoyment and saying, "Yeah, thank you honey. Suck it more. I'm really enjoying it. Please give me more. I love you. You're simply the best wife. I love you with all my heart. Yes! Yes!! Yes!!! I'm about to ejaculate." She left the penis, and he ejaculated.

They got into the bedroom, and she positioned herself in the traditional *Missionary-style sex position,* which is face-to-face with the woman under, and they started caressing and kissing for a while, and then Shaun penetrated her vagina and started making love to her with the new enlarged erected penis. This time around, she could feel a huge difference because there is real contact with her clitoris, which is now stimulating and making her sensational. Mary started screaming out aloud, "Thank you honey. Yeah, give it to me please. Yeah, more, and more. I love it and I love you. Your penis is the perfect size for me. I will love you forever sweetie. You are the best husband in the world," and then he ejaculated and deposited more sperm into her. They both reached orgasm. Exciting!

They disengaged from the missionary style, and she turned to the *Doggy style sex position* and then with full erection, Shaun penetrated her from behind. He started by gently moving his penis in and out, but as she started screaming again for more and more, Shaun was energized, and he increased the speed of his jerking so much that his wife started to respond increasingly so much that they both remained in this position for a long while.

And then they changed again to the *Cowgirl sex position,* which allows Mary to be on top of her husband and face-to-face. She is now in control of the sex session as she continually twists her waist and moves her vagina up and down to make deep contact with Shaun's enlarged penis. This is wonderful and great! They remained in this position until they got tired. They are over the moon on this exciting honeymoon.

The beauty of having sex in different sex-style positions, and in different convenient places in the house, which includes the bedroom, sitting room, and bathroom, is that it provides variety and good memories of the honeymoon for a long time. Don't be a boring soulmate. Don't kill the libido with a bad attitude. Connect fully with your spouse and be enraptured with romance, love, and sex. Create a special lifetime honeymoon paradise for the two of you that will last forever.

One of the things you have to do as a couple is that you must be bold and courageous to initiate romance, love, and sex in your marriage. You are legally married, and this means you are fully licensed to have sex as a couple. Don't leave this function to initiate sex to your husband or wife to do it always. Both of you are one now, and you have right to each other's bodies, and also have the responsibility to initiate romance, love, and sex. You have to quit thinking your spouse will see you as a person who has high libido. Therefore, you will not initiate anything, yet you desire it.

They got into the bathroom together, and had a bath in the Jacuzzi. *The shower Shaun did not want to have with his wife earlier on because of a small penis, he joyfully joined her now.* While they were in the bathroom, they washed each other's bodies, and Shaun was stimulated again as he saw her pointed breasts and nipples and sucked them. He got full erection, and his wife positioned herself again in a doggy style, and he penetrated her from behind and started making love to her while she screamed out for more and more again until they were exhausted. They had their baths and cleaned up. They put on their nightwear and went to the sitting room very delighted with the penis enlargement miracle. Now Mr & Mrs McGregor will fully enjoy their honeymoon. Extraordinary honeymoon in paradise!

The average or normal erection length of a man's penis is in the range of about 5 to 7 inches, with a circumference of about 4.5 to 4.8 inches to give appropriate diameter and girth. But Shaun's full erection penis was just 3 inches long, and a very small girth. The penis was barely visible when it was flaccid because it was tucked inside the scrotum. But God has now done a miracle for him and the length of his penis when fully erected is now 6 inches long with normal increased girth to match.[5-7] The new size of his penis is double the former size, and he is excited and grateful. Our God is a God of double portion and perfection.

Mr and Mrs McGregor had a one-year courtship without sex as Christians who were determined not to fornicate before marriage, but to also keep themselves as pure and holy vessels unto God because they honor and revere God. Shaun did not disclose to Mary that his penis on full erection is just 3 inches long with a small girth. This is still capable of getting a woman pregnant, but there may not be full sexual satisfaction. Shaun was not castrated, therefore he was not a eunuch, and the testicles in his scrotum produce semen well. Will Shaun's non-disclosure of his small penis to Mary before marriage be classified in the category of a case of fraud and deceit?

Is this a Yes, No, or Maybe – Neutral? Will your answer be different if Shaun did not have an erection at all? Thank God for Shaun's penis enlargement miracle.

Shaun said to his wife, "This miracle is worthy of a special thanksgiving offering to God in appreciation. I will do a bank transfer of £1 million pounds into the church account to thank and honor the Lord for this miracle."

Mary said, "God is worthy of all the praise, honor, and thanksgiving. Honey, please do it now."

Shaun immediately transferred one million pounds (£1,000,000.00) into the Shekinah Pentecostal Church account. And he said, "Thank you, Lord Jesus, for this penis enlargement miracle, and for ending this shame and frustration in my life. I am grateful Lord. What medical science could not do for me, you did it in an instant. Ahhh! Lord, I thank you. I will forever be grateful. Now I enjoy sex with my wife, and also enjoy this honeymoon very well. Shame on the devil! All glory be to the Most High God!"

Shaun turned to Mary and said, "I would also like to honor and appreciate the Woman of God, and my special darling wife God used to pray for me for this miracle to happen. I have transferred a hundred thousand pounds (£100,000.00) into your bank account darling. Use it to support your Evangelical ministry work, and buy whatever you like; car, clothes, shoes, bags, perfumes, jewelry. Whatever you like. I love you sweetheart."

When Mary heard that, she was stunned, and she said, "Honey, you shouldn't have bothered on giving me money. It's God that did the miracle. Besides, your money is also my money, and my money is your money. We are one."

Shaun said, "I know all that. But I have already deposited the money into your bank account."

Mary checked her online bank account and saw the £100,000.00. She said to Shaun, "My lord, thank you very much for the money. My God shall supply all your need according to His riches in glory by Christ Jesus. I declare excellent health, wealth, honor, long life, and prosperity for you all the days of your life in Jesus' name. I love you with all my heart darling."

Remember, Sarah called Abraham "My lord" in 1 Peter 3:6. Mary called him "My lord," as a mark of deep respect, and appreciation for the gift.

Shaun affirmed the prayer and said a very big, "Ameeeeeen!" He held her and kissed her and said, "You deserve even more. I know you are my wife, but I also know very well that you are a Woman of God. I will always respect and honor your office as an Evangelist."

Immediately, Mary also did a bank transfer of £15,000.00 into Shekinah Pentecostal Church bank account as a special thanksgiving offering to the Lord for the miracle He did for them. She said, "Heavenly Father, thank you for the penis enlargement miracle you did for me and my husband. I am thankful and grateful. Now we enjoy sex, our honeymoon, and marriage very well. Thank you, Jesus."

It suddenly dawned on Mary that part of the reason why they experienced this penis enlargement miracle was because they honored the Word of God not to commit fornication during their courtship which lasted one year. The Bible says in:

1 Samuel 2:30

> *Wherefore the LORD God of Israel saith, I said indeed that thy house, and the house of thy father, should walk before me for ever:* <u>*but now the LORD saith, Be it far from me; for them that honour me I will honour, and they that despise me shall be lightly esteemed*</u>. (Underline mine)

God is still in the business of honoring Christians who honor His Word and abstain from fornication, sin, and evil. Live holy. When you are clean, pure, and holy, with integrity, you become formidable. Don't despise the Word of God. The Bible says in:

Proverbs 13:13

> *Whoso despiseth the word shall be destroyed: but he that feareth the commandment shall be rewarded.*

Mr and Mrs McGregor did not despise the Word of God which says, *"Flee fornication..."* – 1 Corinthians 6:18. The big lie the devil gives is that: "Everybody fornicates." Even if everybody is doing it, determine that you will not join them. Honor and revere God as a child of God. Strictly avoid sexual immorality because it destroys people. Despise the Word of God and you will be destroyed. (See also 1 Corinthians 3:16-17). However, they honored the Word of God, and they were rewarded miraculously with an enlarged normal penis to enjoy their marriage and honeymoon.

They both sat on the sofa chair in the sitting room, next to each other, with her head resting on him, feeling his warmth, and in front of the TV showing *GOD TV* channel. After a while, Shaun and Mary got together to pray, praise, and thank God before they slept. They thanked God for the success of their wedding, for all the people that came, for all the gifts they received, and for a safe journey to the Island of Santorini, Greece. Above all, they thanked God for the miracle of the penis enlargement. They sang a few songs and prayed in tongues, and ended their prayer. They went straight to bed, held each other, kissed and said, "Good night, and sweet dreams," and slept off.

CHAPTER TWO

DAY 2 – MONDAY
INTIMACY WITH THE HOLY SPIRIT &
INTIMACY IN MARRIAGE

Mr & Mrs McGregor woke up refreshed and strong. It's Christmas and Boxing Day. Shaun greeted his wife, "Honey, good morning."

Mary replied, "Good morning darling. How was your night?"

Shaun answered, "Fine. I thank God that I am alive and well." They embraced each other and got into the bathroom, and brushed their teeth and tongues. They brought out their Bibles and notebooks and got together to do their morning devotion. This has been their way of life right from their courtship days. So this is a good habit they have already developed. They are determined that God will always be at the center of their marriage. Therefore, they will always put God first in all they do. They honor and reverence Him, thank Him, praise, worship, and adore Him always. Hallelujah!

Shaun led her in the praise and worship session, and afterward they made scriptural declarations, and then got into speaking in tongues. It's now time for the teaching of the Word of God to encourage one another, and Shaun said, "Woman of God, can you please give a teaching on the topic: Intimacy with the Holy Spirit, and Intimacy in marriage?"

Mary replied, "You are my husband and head. Please start the teaching on this honeymoon."

But Shaun insisted and said, "I have given you the permission to do it today darling. Tomorrow, I will do the teaching."

And Mary said, "Thank you my lord for giving me the permission to teach today," and she started her teaching by saying:

"INTIMACY WITH THE HOLY SPIRIT, AND INTIMACY IN MARRIAGE

What is intimacy?

Intimacy is a very close friendship, familiarity, or companionship with a person. On a deeper level, it also means love making, sexual intercourse, or copulation with a person in a relationship. To achieve intimacy involves fellowship or communion and this is called *Koinonia* in Greek. To achieve intimacy involves you having a heart of love, powered by faith, in a peaceful location and atmosphere, with constant communication, and your desire to yield to the Holy Spirit.

Intimacy with the Holy Spirit does not just happen. It takes a process, and as Christians, Jesus Christ is our *pattern* to follow.

Jesus was conceived by the power of the Holy Spirit – Luke 1:35; He was filled with the Holy Spirit after John baptized Him – Matthew 3:16-17; He was led by the Holy Spirit into the wilderness in isolation to be tempted by the devil while He fasted for 40 days – Luke 4:1-2;

afterward, he returned into Galilee in the power of the Holy Spirit – Luke 4:14. This process Jesus Christ went through enabled Him to operate supernaturally, and also have continuous deep intimacy with the Holy Spirit, and God the Father – Trinity or Godhead.

Bearing this process and pattern in mind, anyone who desires intimacy with the Holy Spirit must also pay the price and follow the pattern in order to grow spiritually and become a mature Christian.

You must be a born-again Christian. Jesus declared in:

John 3:5-7

> ⁵ *Jesus answered, Verily, verily, I say unto thee, Except a man be born of <u>water </u>and of the <u>Spirit</u>, he cannot enter into the kingdom of God.*
>
> ⁶ *That which is born of the <u>flesh is flesh</u>; and that which is born of the <u>Spirit is spirit</u>.*
>
> ⁷ *Marvel not that I said unto thee, <u>Ye must be born again</u>.* (Underline mine)

Jesus said in verse 7 above, "…*Ye must be born again.*" To become a born-again Christian is a non-negotiable condition you must satisfy in order to have intimacy with the Holy Spirit, and this will also enhance intimacy in marriage.

This born-again thing is achieved through salvation prayer confession – See Romans 10:9-10 and Ephesians 2:8-9. When you declare the salvation confession prayer by faith, a mystery and miracle happens that will activate your Adam sin flesh nature to have the

28

indwelling of the Holy Spirit, with a regenerated or recreated spirit. See verse 6 above, Psalm 51:5, and Romans 3:23. When you make this salvation confession by faith, Jesus comes to dwell in you. *"... Christ **in** you, the hope of glory:"* – Colossians 1:27. The Bible says in:

1 Corinthians 6:17, "But he that is joined unto the Lord is one spirit."

1 John 5:12

> *He that hath the Son hath life; and he that hath not the Son of God hath not life.*

Romans 8:9

> *But ye are not in the <u>flesh</u>, but in the <u>Spirit</u>, if so be that the Spirit of God dwell in you. Now if any man have not the Spirit of Christ, he is none of his.*

Galatians 5:16

> *This I say then, <u>Walk in the Spirit</u>, and ye shall not fulfil the <u>lust of the flesh</u>.*

Galatians 5:25

> *If we live in the <u>Spirit</u>, let us also walk in the <u>Spirit</u>.* (Underline mine)

You have to do water baptism. Jesus did it and also commanded us to do it in Mathew 28:19. What a lot of people do is that after they receive salvation, they remain there doing nothing to grow as a born-again Christian. So they remain stagnated, being a carnal or sensual Christian, and never growing to become a mature spiritual Christian. What do you do to grow? The Bible says in:

1 Peter 2:2

> *As newborn babes, desire the sincere milk of the word, that ye may grow thereby:*

As stated in the above scripture, you must desire, hunger, and be sincere to grow. To make this happen, you have to get a good study Bible, and deliberately and intentionally start doing a methodical Bible study, and meditation on the Word of God to enable you to start growing. You also have to join a good Bible teaching church and start doing other spiritual exercises which includes prayers, praise, worship, thanksgiving, listening to teachings and preaching on the internet by good Ministers of God, reading very good Christian books in various areas including, prayers, Holy Spirit, marriage, giving, prosperity, purpose in life, visions etc. Join a department in the church and become a very active, dedicated member in the vineyard of the Lord, and support and promote the Kingdom of God with your tithes and offerings. You also have to abstain from evil deeds and sin because this grieves the Holy Spirit.

When we receive salvation, Christ dwells in us, and the Holy Spirit interacts with our human spirit and the fruit of the Spirit is activated to start growing and with our cooperation it matures. The Holy Spirit works in us and through us to others. The fruit is singular, not plural as in fruits. It is one fruit with nine parts embedded in it. The Bible says in:

Galatians 5:22-23

> ²² *But the fruit of the Spirit is love, joy, peace, longsuffering, gentleness, goodness, faith,*

> ²³ *Meekness, temperance: against such there is no law.*

The primary reason for the 9 fruit of the Holy Spirit in the life of a believer is to help him grow and mature with good character and habits to become Christ-like. The Bible says in: *Matthew 7:20, "Wherefore by their fruits ye shall know them."* The kind of fruit and lifestyle a Christian manifest is a reflection of what's going on inside them, and the extent of their growth, and maturity.

Infilling of the Holy Spirit: As you do all these, you have to also ensure you are filled with the Holy Spirit or baptism of the Holy Spirit with evidence of speaking in tongues.

Acts 2:4

> *And they were all <u>filled with the Holy Ghost,</u> and <u>began to speak with other tongues,</u> as the Spirit gave them utterance.*

Acts 19:6

> *And when Paul had laid his hands upon them, the <u>Holy Ghost came on them</u>; and <u>they spake with tongues,</u> and prophesied.* (Underline mine)

You must seek to be filled with the Holy Spirit after you have received indwelling of the Holy Spirit as a result of the salvation confession prayer by faith. To be filled with the Holy Spirit, you can ask a Minister of God operating in that dimension or gift to lay hands on you to be filled with the Holy Spirit for you to speak in tongues even as the Apostle Paul did in Acts 19:6 above. You can also ask God to fill you up, even as the scripture says in:

Luke 11:13

> *If ye then, being evil, know how to give good gifts unto your children: how much more shall your heavenly <u>Father give the Holy Spirit to them that ask him</u>?* (Underline mine)

If you are not filled with the Holy Spirit, ask God now to fill you up to saturation and overflow so that you will be quickened to speak in tongues. You also have to desire and hunger to be filled with the Holy Spirit and speak in tongues to enable this to happen.

Holy Spirit empowerment: The Christian life is a journey that involves conscientious commitment. While salvation, indwelling, and infilling of the Holy Spirit can be achieved through confession, and tarrying, Holy Spirit empowerment requires that you truly pay a price for this. Jesus had to be led by the Holy Spirit into the wilderness in isolation for 40 days to be tempted by the devil. For you to be empowered by the anointing of the Holy Spirit also demands that you will be in isolation for a period of time in line with the pattern.

This is a time of crushing, squeezing, and stretching for a believer who desires Holy Spirit anointing for empowerment. God will work on your heart. The Bible says in:

Ezekiel 36:26-27

> ²⁶ *A new heart also will I give you, and a new spirit will I put within you: and I will take away the stony heart out of your flesh, and I will give you an heart of flesh.*
>
> ²⁷ *And I will put my spirit within you, and cause you to walk in my statutes, and ye shall keep my judgments, and do them.* (Underline mine)

The above scripture tells us that man has a stony heart. Part of what God will do during the period of isolation is to crush you, and pass you through brokenness, to humble and transform you and give you a heart of flesh and a new spirit.

Jeremiah 17:9-10

> ⁹ *The heart is deceitful above all things, and desperately wicked: who can know it?*
>
> ¹⁰ *I the LORD search the heart, I try the reins, even to give every man according to his ways, and according to the fruit of his doings.* (Underline mine)

The above scripture also tells us that man is deceitful and desperately wicked. Part of what God will do during the period of isolation is to crush you, and pass you through brokenness, to humble and transform you and give you a heart of flesh and a new spirit. The love of God will be shed abroad your heart by the Holy Spirit. See Romans 5:5.

This process will further involve forsaking all things. Jesus said in:

Luke 14:33

> *So likewise, whosoever he be of you that <u>forsaketh</u> not all that he hath, he cannot be my disciple.* (Underline mine)

There has to be total surrender to God for evolvement and transformation to truly happen. This is a time where God will separate you from worldly activities, and lifestyle. See 1 John 2:15-17. God will also cut you off from a lot of relationships including family and friends who may be a hindrance to your transformation, and anointing of Holy Spirit empowerment. Paul says in *1 Corinthians 15:31 "... I die daily."* You will also die daily to bad habits, bad character, and ungodly things.

John 12:24

> *Verily, verily, I say unto you, Except a corn of wheat fall into the ground and die, it abideth alone: but if it die, it bringeth forth much fruit.*

Galatians 2:20

> *I am crucified with Christ: nevertheless I live; yet not I, but Christ liveth in me: and the life which I now live in the flesh I live by the faith of the Son of God, who loved me, and gave himself for me.*

Deuteronomy 32:39

> *See now that I, even I, am he, and there is no god with me: I kill, and I make alive; I wound, and I heal: neither is there any that can deliver out of my hand.*

1 Peter 5:10

> *But the God of all grace, who hath called us unto his eternal glory by Christ Jesus, after that ye have suffered a while, make you perfect, stablish, strengthen, settle you.*

Surely, one of the things we don't like in life is to go through suffering and pain. But the above scripture says that after we have suffered for a while, God will make us perfect, establish, strengthen, and settle us. It is pressure before pleasure. No test, no testimony. No suffering, crushing, squeezing, stretching, and pain, will also mean no anointing of the Holy Spirit empowerment.

I went through this process of trials, pruning, suffering, and crushing. I lost my job as a Senior Marketing Officer at the Elohim Car Company. I had fibroids, breast cancer with a lump, and I lost my boyfriend, Alan Brown, in a plane crash. Theophilus Anderson, alias *"Commotion,"* hacked into Apex bank accounts and all my entire life savings of £300,000.00 was stolen. I was fully devoted to the Lord, and to the Shekinah Pentecostal Church activities as I joined the choir, and evangelized winning souls, plus hospital visits and praying for patients at the Shalom University Teaching Hospital (SUTH). The crushing was tough, but His amazing grace was sufficient for me to triumph.

I thank God for all-round victory at last. Everything the devil stole from me was restored plus much more. Glory be to God. Hallelujah!

Psalm 34:19

> *Many are the afflictions of the righteous: but the LORD delivereth him out of them all.*

God Himself will ensure you die before He will empower you with the anointing of the Holy Spirit. Jesus passed through this suffering process in the wilderness for 40 days, in the garden of Gethsemane, on the cross of Calvary, died, and resurrected, and He is now seated in heaven in glory with the Father.

Acts 10.38

> *How God anointed Jesus of Nazareth with the Holy Ghost and with power: who went about doing good, and healing all that were oppressed of the devil; for God was with him.*

God will anoint you with the Holy Ghost and power as He did for Jesus our pattern. But, it will also involve the process I have just described. This will further help launch you into the supernatural realm and enable you to start having more *intimacy* with the Holy Spirit, and doing more exploits for the kingdom of God. You will start having more interactions with the Holy Spirit. Hearing from God more, and seeing into the realm of the spirit, and doing, and experiencing, extraordinary blessings and miracles of the Holy Spirit.

2 Corinthians 13:14

> *The grace of the <u>Lord Jesus Christ</u>, and the <u>love of God</u>, and the <u>communion</u> of the <u>Holy Ghost</u>, be with you all. Amen.* (Underline mine)

When you go through the above process I just described, you will be deeply connected with the trinity or Godhead as you commune with the Holy Spirit intimately. This fellowship is called *Koinonia* in Greek. Intimacy with the Holy Spirit will cause you to soar like an eagle. You will be in constant communication with the Holy Spirit full of wisdom, anointing, and His consciousness. Praise God!

INTIMACY IN MARRIAGE

When you understand, and have a good relationship, and intimacy with the Holy Spirit, intimacy in marriage also becomes easy to understand, enjoyable, and fulfilling.

In order to achieve intimacy in marriage, it is important to be joined together with a God ordained, born-again, Holy Spirit filled, tongue talking spouse. In the beginning, God created Adam, and Eve was made from the rib taken from Adam. See Genesis 2:21-23.

Genesis 2:24

> *Therefore shall a man leave his father and his mother, and shall cleave unto his wife: and they shall be <u>one flesh</u>.* (Underline mine)

This oneness is important from the beginning so that a couple will have a legally recognized marriage. This will also help to promote agreement, unity, and intimacy.

Amos 3:3 says, "Can two walk together, except they be agreed?"

It takes agreement for a couple to walk together and have intimacy in marriage. The Bible says in:

Ephesians 5:21-25

> [21] *Submitting yourselves one to another in the fear of God.*
>
> [22] *Wives, submit yourselves unto your own husbands, as unto the Lord.*
>
> [23] *For the husband is the head of the wife, even as Christ is the head of the church: and he is the saviour of the body.*
>
> [24] *Therefore as the church is subject unto Christ, so let the wives be to their own husbands in every thing.*
>
> [25] *Husbands, love your wives, even as Christ also loved the church, and gave himself for it;*

Verse 21 above makes it clear that Christians, including couples, should submit to one another in the fear of God. Apostle Paul was addressing the whole church here. Apply wisdom, and submit as the Holy Spirit leads, both to those in authority, peers, and even your subordinates, as a mark of respect, humility, and to also foster peace and prosperity.

Verses 22-24 *specifically* says wives should submit to their own husbands as they would submit to *Jesus Christ and in everything*. Therefore, before you rebel against your husband on any matter as a wife, ask yourself if you will rebel against our Lord Jesus on that same matter. If not, then submit.

Verse 25 also *specifically* says husbands should love their wives as Christ loved the church and gave himself for it. Again, as a husband, if you are not loving your wife as Jesus Christ loved the church and gave Himself for it, then you have to step up your love to the *Agape* love of Christ, which is also unconditional love.

DO EVERYTHING JOINTLY

In order for a couple in a marriage to truly bond and have intimacy, they have to keenly adopt and adapt to the attitude of doing everything jointly. This helps them to be really fused together as one and become inseparable after marriage.

Matthew 19:6

> *Wherefore they are no more twain, but one flesh. What therefore God hath joined together, let not man put asunder.*

There are so many things a couple needs to do jointly that will greatly enhance intimacy in marriage. Let's look at a few of them.

Spiritual exercises: Bible study, scriptural declarations, prayers, thanksgiving, praise, worship, dancing etc. have to be done jointly by the couple because they help with bonding and intimacy in marriage.

Matthew 18:19

> *Again I say unto you, That if two of you shall agree on earth as touching any thing that they shall ask, it shall be done for them of my Father which is in heaven.*

Ecclesiastes 4:9

> *Two are better than one; because they have a good reward for their labour.*

Personal hygiene: Before I talk about sex, I would like to emphasize the importance of cleanliness because this is one factor that can either attract or repel intimacy in marriage. They say, *"Cleanliness is next to Godliness."* Therefore, as a couple, make deliberate efforts to ensure you keep up with personal hygiene. Shower daily, wash your genitals daily, brush your teeth and tongue daily, wear clean clothes, dress your hair properly, cut short your pubic hairs, clean shave for the man, avoid alcohol, drugs, and tobacco smoking as a Christian etc. All these will effectively enhance good breath, closeness, and intimacy with your spouse. Some people may not even enter into a serious relationship with you if they don't find you to be clean and attractive, not to talk of intimacy. For them, it's a No! The Bible says in:

1 Samuel 16:7

> *But the LORD said unto Samuel, Look not on his countenance, or on the height of his stature; because I have refused him: for the LORD seeth not as man seeth; <u>for man looketh on the outward appearance,</u> but the LORD looketh on the heart.* (Underline mine)

The above underlined scripture says, "... *for man looketh on the outward appearance, ...*" Since man looks at the outward appearance, ensure you pay attention to that. Make sure your outward appearance is satisfactory to you, because if you don't take proper care of yourself, it could lead to germs, disease, sickness and poor health. Your outward appearance also has to be satisfactory to your spouse.

When Naomi was planning to connect her daughter-in-law, Ruth, to Boaz, "*...a mighty man of wealth...*" – Ruth 2:1, read the counsel she gave to her in:

Ruth 3:3 – (New International Version (NIV)

> <u>*Wash, put on perfume, and get dressed in your best clothes*</u>. *Then go down to the threshing floor, but don't let him know you are there until he has finished eating and drinking.* (Underline mine)

Naomi said to Ruth in the underlined scripture above, "*Wash, put on perfume, and get dressed in your best clothes...*" Don't appear before your spouse, scruffy and unkempt. It's important to note also that keeping up with your outward appearance and cleanliness should not only be during courtship, because what some people do is that they stop all that when they get married. You must continue to do it to attract intimacy.

Character and attitude: Apart from your outward appearance, a couple must also pay attention to their attitude. Have the right positive attitude and mindset to marriage. Get rid of all repulsive bad habits because they will be a hindrance to intimacy. Don't kill the excitement and libido with a repugnant attitude and behavior. For example, improve your way of communication because the Bible says in:

1 Corinthians 15:33

> *Be not deceived: evil communications corrupt good manners.*

Note that your communication is not only about what you say but also includes your facial expressions, gestures, body language, and the way you do things generally. Communicate well with your attitude.

Conducive environment: The Holy Spirit is a gentle Spirit, and He operates best in a peaceful atmosphere. Avoid a troublesome, chaotic environment. We are created in the image and likeness of God. Therefore, a couple has to make a deliberate effort to create a conducive environment to live in. Play very good deep spiritual praise and worship songs or scriptures on audio because they help to promote a conducive atmosphere for intimacy. Ensure that you live in a clean, welcoming, conducive place, especially your bedroom. This factor also has a way of promoting intimacy in marriage, because cleanliness is next to godliness.

Electronic gadgets: Completely or significantly avoid excessive use of electronic gadgets like mobile phones, tablets, computer laptops, TV, office files, social media activities etc. when you are in the bedroom with your spouse. This can be a serious distraction, and a barrier hindering intimacy. Besides, it is also disrespectful to your spouse to do that. Instead, focus on your spouse and share jokes together, laugh together, kiss and cuddle one another while in the bedroom in order to create excitement and libido.

Foreplay: This is a very essential aspect of stirring up your spouse for a sexual relationship. Sex should be seen as something beyond physical contact. Sex is an effective connection of the couple physically, emotionally, and spiritually. This means that there has to be genuine heart-to-heart connections through kissing, cuddling, touching, rubbing, massaging of different parts of the body. As your spouse touches your erogenous zones, tell them those parts you like or don't like so that they will know whether to repeat it or not. When foreplay is done by a couple, they can proceed to have intercourse and also have orgasm. Love and intimacy grow when a couple sincerely stay committed to a meaningful foreplay.

Sexual intercourse: This is very vital for a legally married couple because it will greatly help for bonding and intimacy. Sexual intercourse is a ***must*** to achieve a deeper level of intimacy in marriage. Have sex daily if you can, but do not defraud or deny your spouse sex. To do so will not help with intimacy, but will rather tear the marriage apart.

1 Corinthians 7:1-5

> [1] *Now concerning the things whereof ye wrote unto me: It is good for a man not to touch a woman.*

> [2] *Nevertheless, to avoid fornication, let every man have his own wife, and let every woman have her own husband.*

> [3] *Let the husband render unto the wife due benevolence: and likewise also the wife unto the husband.*

> [4] *The wife hath not power of her own body, but the husband: and likewise also the husband hath not power of his own body, but the wife.*

> [5] *Defraud ye not one the other, except it be with consent for a time, that ye may give yourselves to fasting and prayer; and come together again, that Satan tempt you not for your incontinency.*

Note that sexual intimacy is far beyond physical body contact and closeness. For a couple to achieve sexual intimacy, they must be wholeheartedly involved and connected spirit, soul, and body, and it is this sincere sexual act that produces the mystery of oneness in a marriage. Real sexual intimacy can only be achieved when a couple is fully involved and connected physically, emotionally, and spiritually in a loving relational marriage. Avoid being distracted by silly thoughts of a former partner, pornographic images, to reply to a text, to go to the shop etc. while you are with your spouse making love. Don't be absent-minded. Be conscious of what is happening, participate, and enjoy every moment very well.

During sexual intercourse, the couple has to totally surrender to one another. No holding back of your positive emotions of love, joy, and excitement. Yield and cooperate with your spouse to make this moment enjoyable and fantastic.

Sex is absolutely vital for intimacy in marriage. When a couple completely excludes sex from their marriage, bonding and intimacy will be greatly affected, and the marriage will be as good as dead. Simply put, *"No sex, no marriage."* The only time a couple is permitted to have a sex break is a period of fasting and prayer, and that should also be with consent. See verse 5 above.

While we are on this matter of sex, it is important to be fully committed to your marriage, remaining very loyal, without committing adultery. *Adultery* is a work of the flesh. See Galatians 5:19-21 list. Therefore, discipline yourself, and don't break your marriage vow not to cheat. Do not betray the trust your spouse has in you. It is disrespectful, wickedness, and a sin to commit adultery. Apostle Paul counselled us in:

Galatians 5:16

> *This I say then, Walk in the Spirit, and ye shall not fulfil the lust of the flesh.*

The sin of adultery is so serious to the extent that Jesus had to clearly state this:

Matthew 5:28

> *But I say unto you, That whosoever looketh on a woman to lust after her hath committed adultery with her already in his heart.*

From the above scripture you can see that you don't only have to *actually* commit adultery to be guilty. When a man *looks* at a woman *lustfully* with the *intention* of making love to her, he is also deemed to have committed adultery with the woman in his heart. Brethren, beware! Adultery is not the work of the devil. Discipline yourself. Many Christians wrongly accuse the devil for this sin. Read what King Solomon said in:

Proverbs 6:32-33

> *32 But whoso committeth adultery with a woman lacketh understanding: he that doeth it destroyeth his own soul.*

> *33 A wound and dishonour shall he get; and his reproach shall not be wiped away.*

The above scripture clearly states the consequence of adultery – self-destruction!

Sleep on the same bed, live in the same room, and house: In order to deeply achieve intimacy in marriage, it is absolutely essential that the couple should live in the same house, stay in the same room, and share the same bed daily. This will give the couple the opportunity to talk, cuddle, have sex, and connect more intimately in all areas of their marriage. There must not be any flimsy excuse not to satisfy this aspect of marriage. Not even riches, poverty, old age, or a quarrel should make a couple not sleep on the same bed.

Ephesians 4:26-27

> [26] *Be ye angry, and sin not: let not the sun go down upon your wrath:*

> [27] *Neither give place to the devil.*

The above scripture says that even if a couple quarreled and is angry, they have to settle it before sunset. Reconcile on the bed with good sex and laughter so that the devil will not be able to come in to spoil the marriage.

Communication: The way a couple communicates must change after marriage because it will help with intimacy. Your mode of communication has to change from singular to plural. For example, it now has to be *our, we, us* instead of *I, my, me, mine.* It has to be ***our*** money, car, house, and not ***my*** money, car or house. The way you speak will either repel or promote intimacy.

One of the ways to maintain communion and intimacy with the Holy Spirit is to be in constant communication with Him. Also be in constant communication with your spouse because it will help achieve intimacy. Call, text, email, WhatsApp, send a card, etc. to your spouse. Just send them one line like:

I love you.
I miss you. I desire to have you beside me.
I'm longing to see you.
I am thinking of you every moment.
You mean to me more than words can express.
When I set my eyes on you tonight I will devour you.

Surely, these sorts of positive text messages can act as a catalyst and booster to stir up your spouse. Try it!

Also ensure you don't provoke your spouse to anger by cursing, criticizing, belittling, and snubbing them. Avoid evil and corrupt communication.

Ephesians 4:29

> *Let no corrupt communication proceed out of your mouth, but that which is good to the use of edifying, that it may minister grace unto the hearers.*

1 Corinthians 15:33

> *Be not deceived: evil communications corrupt good manners.*

Learn to always speak to your spouse in a gentle, calm, and loving manner. Avoid raising your voice.

Proverbs 15:1

> *A soft answer turneth away wrath: but grievous words stir up anger.*

Colossians 4:6

> *Let your speech be alway with grace, seasoned with salt, that ye may know how ye ought to answer every man.*

Joint bank account: A Joint bank account operated by honest, fair, transparent, trustworthy couple will help promote intimacy in marriage. However, if one is a reckless spender, and the other a stingy saver, a partial joint account still has to be set up to take care of certain expenditures, or emergencies, while they still operate their personal accounts. Work out the best financial strategy for savings and expenditure that best suits you as a couple.

Always have it in your consciousness that you are one because that will help promote love, trust, peace, and progress. Why do you have to defraud your loved one? To do so is to hurt yourself because both of you are now joined together to become one.

Joint mortgage: It is better for a couple to have a joint mortgage house because it will also help with intimacy in marriage. For a couple to live apart, and not under the same roof, will not promote intimacy in marriage. Always have it in your consciousness that you are one because that will help promote love, trust, peace, and progress.

Eating: When a couple eats together daily, it also has a way of bringing them together intimately. This is a time the husband should sincerely appreciate the wife for cooking delicious meals. The couple can also use this time to relax, calm down, have eye contact, smile and maybe have a little talk.

Shower: The couple should also take a shower together daily and see each other's nakedness. It gives you the opportunity to praise one another's attractive body and physique. Wash each other's bodies. Laugh and chat together. The bathroom can also be a very good place to make love in order to add to your romantic memories.

Outdoor activities: As much as possible, Mr and Mrs should jointly do the gym physical exercise together, take a walk together and hold hands, go to parties and dance together, concerts, theatres, camping, retreats and other outdoor activities, because it will help to bring intimacy in marriage.

Third parties in marriage

One of the things that can lead to separation and divorce in a marriage is when attention is diverted from your spouse and now focused more on external toxic third parties, no matter who they may be. Use wisdom, and the leading of the Holy Spirit to accommodate and maintain good and beneficial third-party relationships. Always remember you are one with your spouse, and therefore, focus more on them. Be mindful of what you say and do about your marriage. Be mindful also of what third parties say and that you listen to and act upon. You could be deceived by envious third parties. Adam and Eve were fine in their marriage until the serpent came and deceived Eve, and they started having problems. See Genesis chapter 3. Avoid gossip. Instead, read your Bible, meditate, pray, thank, praise, and worship God.

There is a reward for doing things jointly as couple

King Solomon, a very wise man, said in:

Ecclesiastes 4:9

> *Two are better than one; because they have a good reward for their labour.*

The above scripture is a counsel given by a wise man that will always be true. Therefore, no matter what happens to you as a couple, determine in advance that separation and divorce to be alone will never be an option. Always stick together like superglue. Inseparable! Why? There is always a good reward for the labor of a committed couple who stay together. Let's also look at what King Solomon said in the next verse.

Ecclesiastes 4:10

> *For if they fall, the one will lift up his fellow: but woe to him that is alone when he falleth; for he hath not another to help him up.*

The above verse further emphasizes the danger of not being together and doing things jointly. When a couple is together, they support one another, but woe to him that is alone. Do everything jointly as a couple.

Forgiveness: Couples must have the merciful attitude of forgiving their spouse, and avoid grudges and malice. When a couple does not forgive easily and quickly, it will affect intimacy in marriage.

Ephesians 4:32

> *And be ye kind one to another, tenderhearted, forgiving one another, even as God for Christ's sake hath forgiven you.*

Love: As Christians, we are to love one another. Jesus gave us this new commandments in:

John 13:34-35

> [34] *A new commandment I give unto you, That ye love one another; as I have loved you, that ye also love one another.*

> [35] *By this shall all men know that ye are my disciples, if ye have love one to another.*

What is love? The Apostle Paul gave the meaning of love in:

1 *Corinthians 13:4-8 (New International Version – (NIV)*

> [4] *Love is patient, love is kind. It does not envy, it does not boast, it is not proud.*

> [5] *It does not dishonor others, it is not self-seeking, it is not easily angered, it keeps no record of wrongs.*

> [6] *Love does not delight in evil but rejoices with the truth.*

> [7] *It always protects, always trusts, always hopes, always perseveres.*

> [8] *Love never fails. But where there are prophecies, they will cease; where there are tongues, they will be stilled; where there is knowledge, it will pass away.*

There are so many things that can help enhance intimacy in marriage apart from the above points discussed. However, that's all I have to say for now on this subject. My prayer is that we will continually be filled with the

Holy Spirit, and be in constant communion, intimacy with Him, and also have intimacy in our marriage in Jesus' name. Amen!

Holy Spirit, we invite you. We welcome you. Come and fill us up afresh.
Holy Spirit, fill us, and saturate us to overflow.
Holy Spirit, we love you. Have your way in every area of our lives.
Holy Spirit, fight all our battles, seen and unseen, known and unknown.
Holy Spirit, comfort us, strengthen us, empower us, and fill us up continually in Jesus' name. Amen!"

As soon as she finished teaching, Shaun said "Ameeeeen!" and stood up and started clapping for his wife, and also laughing, filled with the joy of the Lord. He kissed her and lifted her up in the manner he did at the wedding yesterday, and she started laughing out aloud uncontrollably.

Shaun said, "That was a very powerful, anointed message you just preached on a very important subject, and I am very blessed to listen to your teaching. I pray for you that the Lord will replenish you with more grace, wisdom, and anointing in Jesus' name." And she said, "Amen!"

Shaun now said to her, "Honey, can I ask a question?"
Mary replied, "Yes, you can, darling."

QUESTION

Shaun asked, "What will happen to a couple who are not committed to having intimacy with the Holy Spirit, and intimacy in their marriage?"

ANSWER

Mary answered, "That's a very good question, and I would like to start by saying that to have intimacy with the Holy Spirit, and intimacy in marriage does not just happen. You have to deliberately and intentionally be committed to doing the right things, as I have shared in my teaching, to align with the Holy Spirit and also have intimacy in marriage. You must have that positive attitude as a couple to work things out in your marriage. If you don't do anything as a couple, sadly, you will not achieve intimacy. Pay the price and be committed to your marriage, and you will be greatly blessed."

Shaun said, "Thank you, darling, for that brilliant answer."

With this, they ended their morning devotion, and went straight into the bathroom to take a shower. As soon as they saw each other's nakedness, they were both aroused and Shaun got a full erection, and he got close to her and said, "You are so beautiful, so sweet, and I love you." And she said, "I love you too." He started kissing her and fondling her pointed soft breasts. And after a while, she positioned herself in a doggy style, and they started making love and the jerking and screaming went wild and crazy until he ejaculated, and they disengaged as they are both tired, and they cleaned up and had a shower.

As soon as they came out of the bathroom, Mary put on the gospel songs playlist of *Don Moen* starting with the track *Thank You Lord*. And they got dressed and got ready to go to the restaurant for their breakfast.

They came out of their suite and saw the beautiful sunshine and blue, white sky, the beautiful sea view, rocks, plus the refreshing gentle air.

Mary said, "Santorini Island is beautiful."

And Shaun replied, "Yes, it is beautiful indeed. You will get to see more soon."

Mary said, "I can't wait."

Shaun replied, "We are in it already."

They carried on walking towards the Perfecto 5-star restaurant and holding hands. When they got in, they were immediately welcomed by one of the restaurant staff, a beautiful young lady, who smiled and said, "Kalimera," which means, "Good morning."

And they replied "Kalimera."

She said again, "το όνομά μου είναι Οφηλία" which means, "My name is Ophelia."

And they replied, " Ο κύριος και η κυρία McGregor," which means "Mr and Mrs McGregor."

There are varieties of good food in Fira, Island of Santorini, Greece. They moved around the table seeing different prepared continental food, but they settled for the English breakfast they are used to for now. They will try out something new and different, maybe at lunch or dinner. However, the aroma and tantalizing sight of the food is irresistible.

Ophelia said, "It's a buffet. Please serve yourselves and enjoy the meal." This is translated in Greek as, "Είναι μπουφές. Παρακαλούμε να σερβίρετε τον εαυτό σας και να απολαύσετε το γεύμα."

They said, "Efcharisto." So they served sausages, scrambled eggs, bacon, tomatoes, mushrooms, baked beans, and toast. They also got tea, orange juice, mango juice, and water.

They settled down beside each other while they listened to the Christian gospel songs playlist by *Michael W. Smith* playing on the background, and the track *Agnus Dei* is playing at the moment.

Shaun prayed, saying, "Heavenly Father, we thank you for this food. We bless and sanctify it. I declare that as we eat, we will enjoy it, and it will nourish our body. We also ask that you bless the chef and the kitchen staff that prepared the food. Thank you, Jesus." And they both said, "Amen!"

Shaun took some of the scrambled eggs and fed her and gently touched her back, and she said, "This is sweet. Thanks darling." And he said, "You are welcome," and they carried on eating.

When they finished eating, they both agreed that the food was luscious. Mary said, "This Perfecto Restaurant is beautiful, clean, scrumptious food, and good service." Shaun replied, "Yes!" They stood up to leave and said to Ophelia, "Thank you very much." And she answered, "Parakalo," and they left for their suite.

When they got inside the suite, Mary said, "Honey, my parents don't know where I am. Can I call them and let them know where I am?"

Shaun replied, "Of course you can sweetheart."

Mary grabbed her mobile and turned it on because it had been off since they left the wedding reception in London. She found loads of text messages, missed phone calls, many voicemail messages, WhatsApp, Facebook, Instagram, and email messages, but she ignored all that and went straight and called her dad, Chief Police Superintendent Paul Jenkins.

She got through, and she spoke saying, "Hello Dad!"

He answered, "Hello sweetheart. It's good to hear your voice. We've been expecting your call. Where are you now?"

Mary replied, "I am in Fira, on the Island of Santorini, Greece. Very beautiful Island. That's where my darling husband brought me for our 2-week honeymoon, and I am enjoying it daddy."

Paul said, "Tell me about it young lady. I can tell you love it from your voice and tone. Congratulations sweetheart. My prayer is that the Lord will perfect all that concerns you and your husband in Jesus' name. Please hold on for your mum."

"Amen! Thanks daddy," she replied. And continued, "Mummy, how are you? I am in Fira, on the Island of Santorini, Greece, with my husband."

Brenda replied, "Praise God for that. Please take good care of yourself, and your husband and enjoy your honeymoon. The Lord bless you and preserve you both from all evil in Jesus' name."

Mary said, "Amen! Mummy, I have to go now. Bye for now," and they both ended the call.

Mary immediately put off her mobile phone without attending to any message. They have agreed to be in paradise in a world of their own as they spend this 2-week honeymoon holiday together, and to avoid unnecessary phone distractions.

Mary put on the gospel music playlist of *Cece Winans* and the track *Goodness of God* started playing.

They both sat on the soft upholstery sofa in the sitting room and started cuddling, and kissing. Mary moved her hand down, and she grabbed his penis and said, "Whao! You already have a full erection," and he replied, "Yes oh! I'm alive."

As they carried on caressing, they were both aroused and enraptured with love that they couldn't resist making love. He immediately removed her top, unfasted her bra and took it off and held her breasts and started sucking the nipples to arouse her, and she started sighing and moving her body. He stripped her naked as he took off her skirt and lingerie. And he went ahead to take his clothes off. Here they go again. The two excited love birds connected again in copulation, digging it out on this exciting honeymoon. They are in the doggy-style sex position, and Mrs McGregor set off with her melodious screams of sex enjoyment utterances, "Yeaaaaah, that's it, I want more. You're getting it right there. Harder please. I love your enlarged penis, and I love you very much." And he started moving his penis in and out faster and faster as she sighed, and then he ejaculates. And they are now fatigued. They went into the bathroom and cleaned up again.

For Mr and Mrs McGregor, speaking out during their sex sessions is part of a true expression to your spouse that you are really enjoying the sex, and the honeymoon, and this is inspiring for your soulmate to do more. Some people will never express they are enjoying sex whether verbally, or through physical body movements. They will just lay on the bed like a log of wood, giving the impression they don't want sex and they are not enjoying it. This sort of attitude only kills the honeymoon excitement. Don't be a boring honeymoon spouse. You've got to lively up yourself. Don't be gloomy. Be enraptured with romance, love, and sex. So be joyful and have fun. This is a once-in-a-lifetime honeymoon adventure. Enjoy it to the fullest. Be involved spirit, soul, and body. No pretext, moody, or uninteresting attitude. Real sexual intimacy can only be achieved when a couple is fully involved and connected physically, emotionally, and spiritually.

They went to bed and started relaxing as gospel music by *Ron Kenoly* started playing the track *Lift Him up*. After a little while, they both slept off.

They woke up late in the evening, and decided to go and have a light dinner at the restaurant. After their dinner, they went to the Christian Center where couples and other Perfecto 5-star hotel customers came in to relax by watching movies, have snacks and non-alcoholic drinks, playing indoor games like snooker, chess, draughts, scrabble, cards, ludo etc. and having a chat with their partners and friends. It's fun.

They were there till 9.30 pm chatting and seeing people moving around, and they left for their suite. As soon as they came back to their suite, they changed into their nightwear and put on a bit of their perfumes, prayed and went to bed, kissed each other and slept off.

CHAPTER THREE

DAY 3 – TUESDAY
GENERATIONAL FAMILY &
MARRIAGE PATTERNS

They got up early in the morning, and, as always, they started their morning devotion. Mr and Mrs McGregor certainly believe that the best way to start a day as a couple is to thank, praise, worship God and pray. This is exactly what they are going to do. After they'd done that, Shaun said, "It's my turn today to teach the Word of God, and my topic is:

GENERATIONAL FAMILY, AND MARRIAGE PATTERNS

What is a pattern?

A pattern or a model is something designed to serve as a guide for making things. This means that a pattern is the first to be made for others to follow. As Christians, Jesus Christ is our pattern example to follow. The Bible says in:

Genesis 1:28

> *And God blessed them, and God said unto them, Be fruitful, and multiply, and replenish the earth, and subdue it: and have dominion over the fish of*

the sea, and over the fowl of the air, and over every living thing that moveth upon the earth.

Right from the beginning, God created man to have dominion and to operate in generational blessings. Hence, the above scripture says, *"And God blessed them, …"* However, man had an encounter with the serpent which led to the perversion of the original established blessings pattern of God for man.

A pattern can be positive or negative, good or bad. Whenever the original pattern is not followed, it becomes negative or bad. Hence, when a negative pattern starts and continues, it also becomes a negative pattern. This message highlights patterns that need to be corrected.

For this purpose, let us look at the generational family lineage patterns and marriages of our patriarchs, Abraham, Isaac, Jacob, and their descendants.

The Bible is against lying

The Bible makes it clear that lying is not good, and there are many scriptural references to support this fact.

Psalm 31:18

Let the lying lips be put to silence; which speak grievous things proudly and contemptuously against the righteous.

Psalm 59:12

For the sin of their mouth and the words of their lips let them even be taken in their pride: and for cursing and lying which they speak.

Psalm 109:2

> *For the mouth of the wicked and the mouth of the deceitful are opened against me:they have spoken against me with a lying tongue.*

Psalm 119:163

> *I hate and abhor lying: but thy law do I love.*

Proverbs 12:22

> *Lying lips are abomination to the LORD: but they that deal truly are his delight.*

The above scriptures condemn lying. To further buttress the fact that lying is bad, Jesus referred to the devil as a liar in John 8:44. Therefore, lying is of the devil. Jesus further said in:

John 8:32

> *And ye shall know the truth, and the truth shall make you free.*

If the truth makes people free, then logically, lies will also make people bound and remain in bondage. Tell the truth and be free.

The lying pattern of the patriarchs

As seen from the above scriptures, lying is not good. However, we also see from the scriptures this generational family pattern to lie in the lives of the patriarchs.

Abraham

Genesis 12:11-13

> ¹¹ *And it came to pass, when he was come near to enter into Egypt, that <u>he said</u> unto <u>Sarai his wife</u>, Behold now, I know that thou art a <u>fair woman</u> to look upon:*

> ¹² *Therefore it shall come to pass, when the Egyptians shall see thee, that they shall say, This is his wife: and they will <u>kill me,</u> but they will save thee alive.*

> ¹³ <u>*Say, I pray thee, thou art my sister*</u>: *that it may be well with me for thy sake; and my soul shall live because of thee.* (Underline mine)

The above scripture tells us that Abraham lied, though he did that to save his life. Abraham repeated the same lie in:

Genesis 20:2

> <u>*And Abraham said of Sarah his wife, She is my sister*</u>: *and Abimelech king of Gerar sent, and took Sarah.* (Underline mine)

The Living Bible says in Exodus 20:16, "*You must not lie.*" It's important to be on the watchout when your spouse tells lies repeatedly, because the devil always capitalizes on lies, no matter how small the lie may be, and lies have consequences when the devil is involved, and repeated lies becomes a pattern.

Isaac

When Abraham lied that Sarah was his sister, Isaac was not yet born. And when Isaac was born, he also lied in:

Genesis 26:6-7

> 6 And <u>Isaac</u> dwelt in Gerar:
>
> 7 And the men of the place asked him of his wife; and <u>he said, She is my sister</u>: for he feared to say, She is my wife; lest, said he, the men of the place should <u>kill me</u> for <u>Rebekah;</u> because she <u>was fair</u> to look upon. (Underline mine)

It is important to note from the above scripture that the exact lie that Abraham told, Isaac, his son, repeated. They both lied and said this about their wives, *"She is my sister."* Like father, like son. This, indeed, is a negative family pattern that must be terminated.

Jacob

When Jacob was born, he also lied. However, he did not lie about his wife, but lied to Isaac, his father, that he was Esau, and deceitfully got his brother's blessing. He was a supplanter and a cheat. See Genesis 27 for the full account of how Jacob lied that he was Esau and deceitfully got his brother's blessing from Isaac.

Conclusion: you can see from the above that there is a generational lying pattern in the family. Grandfather, father, and son lied. As I have already shown above, lying is bad, and such negative patterns must be broken and stopped in the family.

Fair wives pattern

Fair also means beautiful. There is also a pattern in the generational lineage of the patriarchs that shows that they were attracted to fair or beautiful women.

Abraham married a fair wife, *Sarah*. See Genesis 12:11 above.

Isaac married a fair wife, *Rebekah*. See Genesis 26:7 above.

Jacob also married a beautiful wife, *Rachel*. See Genesis 29:17.

The lying pattern of the matriarchs

Apart from the fact that the patriarchs lied, we also see that their wives, the matriarchs, also lied.

Sarah, Abraham's wife, laughed and denied that she laughed. See Genesis 18:12-15.

Rebekah, Isaac's wife, played a manipulative and deceitful role to displace Esau and bring on Jacob to be blessed by Isaac. See Genesis 27.

Rachel, Jacob's wife, covered up Laban's idols and claimed she was observing her menstrual period. See Genesis 31:32-35.

You can see from the above that the matriarchs also lied, and this is a bad generational pattern in the family.

The barrenness pattern of the matriarchs

Sarah, Abraham's wife, was barren for 25 years, according to Bible scholars, before she gave birth to Isaac at the age of 90 years. Abraham was called at the age of 75, and he had Isaac at the age of 100 years.

Rebekah, Isaac's wife, was barren for 20 years. See Genesis 25:20-26.

Rachel, Jacob's wife, was also barren. See Genesis 29:31.

The polygamy pattern of the patriarchs

Abraham married Sarah, Hagar, and Keturah. He also had concubines. They all had children for him.

Isaac was the only one who had one wife, Rebekah.

Jacob married Leah, and Rachel, and his wives' maidservants, Zilpah, and Bilhah also had children with him.

The loss of birthright pattern of the firstborn sons of the patriarchs

There is a generational pattern running in the family whereby the firstborn sons of the patriarchs lost their birthright to their father's inheritance.

Ishmael was Abraham's firstborn, but he lost his birthright to Isaac because he was the son of the bondwoman Hagar, and Isaac was the son of Sarah, promised child. See Genesis 16 and 21.

Esau was Isaac's firstborn, but he lost his birthright to Jacob. See Genesis 25:31-34, and Exodus 4:22.

Rueben was Jacob's firstborn, but he lost his birthright to the sons of Joseph. See 1 Chronicles 5:1.

Manasseh was Joseph's firstborn, but he lost his birthright to Ephraim. See Genesis 48:5 & 17-20.

Common trends of generational patterns in families and marriages

In recent times, we see many types of negative generational patterns and occurrences which includes health, evil, and poverty issues. For example, Medical Science Research has been able to show that certain sicknesses and diseases are hereditary. Sicknesses such as arthritis, breast cancer, fibroids, epilepsy, mental illness, diabetes etc. are known to occur in certain families.

Similar things also happen with social and economic problems like stealing, alcohol drinking, smoking cigarettes, drugs, illiteracy, poor education, unemployment, adultery, divorce etc. Sometimes, these sort of issues come up as generational family pattern occurrences. Like mother, like daughter. See Ezekiel 16:44. Also, like grandfather, like father, and like son. God forbid bad patterns!

At this point, I would like to share my personal experience and testimony about the generational pattern that happened in my family. My grandfather had a small penis, and as a result of this, he gave birth to only my father and his wife divorced him. My father also had a small penis, and as a result of this, he gave birth to only me and his wife divorced him. I also had a small penis before. That was a repeated generational family pattern. Thank God that small penis pattern has now been broken forever in my lineage because I now have a normal enlarged penis after my wife prayed for me on Christmas Day. This is indeed a miracle for me, and I know by the special grace of God, my children will have normal penises, and my marriage will be till death do we part because my wife will not divorce me because of small a penis. This is a very big miracle and testimony for me. Praise God!

The reason why I chose to teach this topic is because I have had experiential knowledge of the generational pattern of small penis in my family lineage and I know how frustrating and painful it can be.

How to end negative generational family patterns

Family investigation

Before you marry, try to ask questions and do investigations about the family you are proposing to join by marriage. Ask questions about any serious issues, and obvious hereditary sickness or disease, mental health problems, evil occurrences, alcoholism, smoking, drug abuse etc.

Prayer

This is a very effective way of ending negative generational patterns. I am a living example to testify that prayer certainly ends it. My wife used a powerful prayer to end the small penis problem for me forever.

Prayer points

- You demon of generational family hereditary sicknesses and disease patterns, I set you ablaze with the Holy Ghost consuming fire to burn to ashes forever in Jesus' name. Amen! Pray! See Hebrews 12:29.
- I visit the foundations of my ancestors and I root out, pull down, and destroy by Holy Ghost fire any existing evil covenant, or altar, causing negative generational family patterns in Jesus' name. Amen! Pray! See Jeremiah 1:10.
- I declare in the name of Jesus, that the power in the blood of Jesus will locate right now and begin to fight, and terminate every family witchcraft attack in Jesus' name. Amen! Pray!
- Every evil arrow, and weapon of the devil, to cause negative generational family patterns, I say back to the sender now in Jesus' name. Amen! Pray!
- Lord, I ask for your forgiveness and mercy to deliver me and my family from all Satanic known and unknown bad generational family patterns in Jesus' name. Amen! Pray!
- I declare all round fruitfulness, blessings, prosperity, and only positive generational blessing patterns in my family in Jesus' name. Amen! Pray!

After the teaching by Shaun, Mary started clapping for her husband and said a very big, "Ameeeeen!," to the teaching and prayers. She continued, "Honey, this teaching is instructional, and inspiring. I am blessed and comforted listening to your teaching. I pray the good Lord will fill you with more wisdom, and the anointing of the Holy Spirit in Jesus' name. Amen!"

Mary said, "Honey, can I ask a question?"

Shaun replied, "Of course you can, darling."

QUESTION

Mary asked, "Honey, how did this small penis issue start in your family lineage? Do you know?"

ANSWER

Shaun answered, "That's a good question. My grandfather told me my great-grandfather committed fornication with a young virgin girl, and denied. The girl's father was angry and cursed my great-grandfather, saying, 'For doing this to my daughter, I declare your penis and those of your generations to come will shrink and dry up.' My great-grandfather's penis shrank. He went back to the girl's father to accept he had done it and beg for forgiveness, but it was too late. That's how the small penis problem started in my family."

Mary said, "Thank you for your answer. It was good you were able to find out how it started. With this additional information, I join my faith with your faith and declare that we cancel and nullify that curse that man placed on your great-grandfather and his lineage in the name of Jesus. I declare that henceforth, you and our children will continually have a normal penis in Jesus' name." Shaun shouted, "Ameeeeeeen!"

Mary continued, "This your great-grandfather's case, is proof that the family generation pattern is real, and we have to live right avoiding sin, in order not to attract it to our life and lineage. Dominic Lloyds, my former Oxford University student had continuous erection problems because he slept with a Caribbean woman and did not fully fulfill the promise he made to the woman, and she inflicted him with voodoo. I prayed for him at the hospital, and God healed him instantly. The lesson to learn here is that we must do our best as believers to continually detest and avoid sin and curse, knowing that the consequence could be generational. God visits the iniquity of fathers as stated in *Exodus 34:7 saying '... visiting the iniquity of the fathers upon the children, and upon the children's children, unto the third and to the fourth generation.'* That's great-grandfather, grandfather, father, and son – 4 generations. Now the curse has been destroyed and stopped forever in Jesus' name. Amen!"

Shaun replied, "Amen! I totally agree with you, Woman of God."

Shaun continued, "To *balance* this teaching, I would like to state here what the Bible also says in:

Ezekiel 18:20

> *The soul that sinneth, it shall die. The son shall not bear the iniquity of the father, neither shall the father bear the iniquity of the son: the righteousness of the righteous shall be upon him, and the wickedness of the wicked shall be upon him.*

As the above scripture states, it is better to believe and hold on to this scripture that, "... *The son shall not bear the iniquity of the father,.."* I think this scripture is about fairness, accountability, and responsibility capable of calling everyone to order, knowing that a man will bear the consequence of his iniquity. Your innocent descendants will not bear the consequences.

2 Corinthians 5:17

> *Therefore if any man be in Christ, he is a new creature: old things are passed away; behold, all things are become new.*

As born-again Christians, we must always have it in our consciousness by faith that negative generational patterns are henceforth canceled, and that we are overcomers, more than conquerors, and victorious in Christ Jesus. Receive salvation now in Jesus' name. Amen!"

This brings to an end their morning devotion.

Mr and Mrs McGregor put on their *Hillsong gospel music* playlist starting with the track *Here I am to Worship*, and they immediately proceeded to the bathroom and had their shower. They dressed up and made their way to the Perfecto restaurant and had their breakfast. They came out of the restaurant and had a walk down the street while holding hands, chatting, and having a proper exterior view of the Perfecto 5-star hotel surroundings, and it was a beautiful view indeed. They saw the ships on the sea, the blue white sky with the radiating bright sunshine.

They came back to their Perfecto 5-star hotel suite, and Shaun put on the gospel playlist of *Hillsong* and the track *I surrender* started playing. They sat down together on the soft upholstered chair in the sitting room.

Shaun said, "Just to let you know, we will be in the gym tomorrow morning for a workout and to engage in fitness activities. We will also be at the museum, and the church tomorrow. I have already arranged for a private tour guide to show us around tomorrow. One more thing, tomorrow is Wednesday, and we will do our fasting as we have always done Wednesdays and Sundays till 6 pm. We will also continue to participate in all the Shekinah Pentecostal Church corporate fasting. No sex during our fasting periods as well. I hope that's all fine with you darling."

Mary replied, "Yes, that's all fine with me darling. Thank you for arranging the tour of the museum, and the church. I am looking forward to that," and she held her husband and kissed him. And Shaun said, "You are welcome darling."

They brought out their scrabble game and played together. They started playing and recorded everything on the score sheets. In the past, Mary won most of the time, so she felt it would be an easy win for her again, but at the end of the game, Shaun won. Mary said, "I can't believe you beat me today." Shaun was happy he won and replied, "You better believe it I won you. The score sheet is there for you to crosscheck." And she said, "Congratulations on this occasion. But get ready because next time, I will beat you." He replied, "OK oh! We shall see."

They both got ready and went down to the restaurant to have their dinner. They decided to try something Greek for the first time. They decided to go for Greek salad, seafood, fish dishes, and pastries. They also got bananas, apples, mango juice, and water.

After their dinner, they went straight back to their suite, sat on the sofa in the sitting room and relaxed while watching the TV tuned to *GOD TV* channel. After a while, they prayed, put on their nightwear, got into bed, kissed, and slept.

CHAPTER FOUR

DAY 4 – WEDNESDAY
THE BENEFITS OF FASTING;
MUSEUM & CHURCH VISIT

Mr and Mrs McGregor woke up in the morning feeling refreshed. They started thanking, praising, and worshiping the Most High God for the gift of life, and for good health. They already have a plan of what to do for the day, and it is helpful to always have a *"To-do list"* because it serves as a reminder and guide. They are fasting today. After the thanksgiving, praise, worship, and prayer session, Mrs McGregor started her teaching for the day on the topic:

THE BENEFITS OF FASTING

Mary said, "I have decided to teach this topic because Jesus commanded that Christians should fast, and He practiced what He preached by fasting 40 days in the wilderness in Matthew 4 and Luke 4. A lot of couples in marriage tend to ignore, or not properly observe this important aspect of spiritual exercise, which has immense benefits not just for couples, but also for the entire Christians in the body of Christ. Since we are fasting today, I would like to use this opportunity to discuss fasting.

What is fasting?

Fasting is simply a period of abstinence from food, drinks, and some other things like sex, the use of mobile phones for calls, the internet and social media, and all ungodly activities either partially or completely. During fasting, you also have to abstain from sin and evil acts. Fasting is also a time where you set yourself apart from worldly influence, which is consecration, and devotion to spiritual exercise.

How to fast

Our Lord Jesus Christ instructed us to fast and also told us how to fast below in:

Matthew 6:16-18

> [16] *Moreover when ye fast, be not, as the hypocrites, of a sad countenance: for they disfigure their faces, that they may appear unto men to fast. Verily I say unto you, They have their reward.*
>
> [17] *But thou, when thou fastest, anoint thine head, and wash thy face;*
>
> [18] *That thou appear not unto men to fast, but unto thy Father which is in secret: and thy Father, which seeth in secret, shall reward thee openly.*

You can see from the above scripture that fasting is not optional for Christians, including couples in marriage. The only reason you may be exempt from fasting is pregnancy, or other medical grounds because of certain health challenges.

Jesus Christ approved fasting for Christians in the above scriptures, saying *"Moreover, when ye fast, ..."* Note that He said, 'When' and not 'If', which means we've got to fast. He said again in *Matthew 17:21*, *"Howbeit this kind goeth not out but by prayer and fasting."* This means there are certain challenges, sicknesses and diseases which can only be conquered by a combination of prayer and fasting.

Spiritual exercise

Fasting alone as a form of spiritual exercise may not suffice. Therefore, for efficiency, effectiveness, and better results, it is advisable to combine fasting with other forms of spiritual exercise like prayers, Bible study, meditations, thanksgiving, praise, and worship. Apart from spiritual exercises, appropriate sacrifice, and a heart of love, backed by faith, helps to guarantee victory.

Appointed time

It is important to note that contrary to some believer's belief, fasting does not always end a challenge, tribulation, or evil immediately. The reason for this is that God has appointed time for certain things to be accomplished, and this means that fasting may not always get you your desired outcome. The Bible says in:

Ecclesiastes 3:1

> *¹ To every thing there is a season, and a time to every purpose under the heaven:*

Ecclesiastes 3:11

> [11] *He hath made every thing beautiful in his time: also he hath set the world in their heart, so that no man can find out the work that God maketh from the beginning to the end.*

The above scriptures tell us that there is a season, and appointed time for God to accomplish things in our life, and He makes all things beautiful in His time, not our time, and fasting may not change this. Besides, we cannot do evil and try to use fasting to reverse it.

For example, in 2 Samuel 12:15-18, King David attempted to use fasting to stop the death of the son Uriah's wife, Bathsheba, gave birth to for him as a result of the adultery he committed with her. However, the child still died on the seventh day of David's fasting.

2 Samuel 12:15-18

> [15] *And Nathan departed unto his house. <u>And the LORD struck the child that Uriah's wife bare unto David, and it was very sick.</u>*

> [16] *David therefore besought God for the child; <u>and David fasted</u>, and went in, and lay all night upon the earth.*

> [17] *And the elders of his house arose, and went to him, to raise him up from the earth: but he would not, <u>neither did he eat bread with them</u>.*

> [18] *<u>And it came to pass on the seventh day, that the child died</u>. And the servants of David feared to tell*

him that the child was dead: for they said, Behold, while the child was yet alive, we spake unto him, and he would not hearken unto our voice: how will he then vex himself, if we tell him that the child is dead? (Underline mine)

From the above scriptures, it is obvious that fasting, even by King David, that God acknowledged to be a man after His own heart, could not stop the death of a newborn baby. This is because King David did evil in the sight of the Lord by committing adultery with Uriah's wife and also plotted the death of Uriah on the battlefield. God was furious and struck the child. God is no respecter of persons. This shows that we must live right as we fast, and avoid adultery and sin which got David into this predicament. Don't deliberately commit adultery or fornication, and then begin to fast for God to forgive you and have mercy. Discipline yourself, and put your flesh in subjection, through the power of the Holy Spirit, as you also reverence God in obedience to His Word.

THE BENEFITS OF FASTING

Fasting humbles us

Psalm 35:13

13 But as for me, when they were sick, my clothing was sackcloth: I humbled my soul with fasting; and my prayer returned into mine own bosom. (Underline mine)

Psalm 69:10

> *10 When I wept, and chastened my soul with fasting, that was to my reproach.* (Underline mine)

In the above scriptures, King David humbled and chastened his soul with fasting. God hates pride. *James 4:6* says, "... *God resisteth the proud, but giveth grace unto the humble.*" Fasting can effectively help to deal with and deliver couples from pride and that will mean less strife in marriage. Humble yourself by fasting.

Fasting can pacify the anger of the Lord to have mercy

King Ahab

1 Kings 21:27-29

> *27 And it came to pass, when Ahab heard those words, that he rent his clothes, and put sackcloth upon his flesh, and fasted, and lay in sackcloth, and went softly.*

> *28 And the word of the LORD came to Elijah the Tishbite, saying,*

> *29 Seest thou how Ahab humbleth himself before me? because he humbleth himself before me, I will not bring the evil in his days: but in his son's days will I bring the evil upon his house.* (Underline mine)

King Ahab killed Naboth and took his vineyard. This displeased the Lord, and He sent Prophet Elijah to tell him that he will also die. The above scripture tells us that when King Ahab heard those words that he will die, he immediately humbled himself with fasting. God saw he was genuinely sorry as he humbled himself with fasting and then transferred the death sentence to his descendants. Can you see why children suffer from generational curses and iniquities their parents committed? As Christians, we have to determine to live life deliberately and consciously avoiding sin, knowing the consequences can be brutal and deadly, not just for the offender but also for the lineage.

Nineveh city

God saw the enormous wickedness happening in the city of Nineveh, and sent Prophet Jonah to go and cry against the city to repent or face destruction. They declared a mandatory fast for all including animals. God saw they humbled themselves and repented, and God had mercy and was pacified not to destroy the city. The Bible says in:

Jonah 3:5-10

> 5 *So the people of <u>Nineveh </u>believed God, and <u>proclaimed a fast,</u> and put on sackcloth, from the greatest of them even to the least of them.*

> 6 *For word came unto <u>the king of Nineveh,</u> and he arose from his throne, and he laid his robe from him, and covered him with sackcloth, and sat in ashes.*

> 7 *And he caused it to be proclaimed and published through Nineveh by the decree of the king and his nobles, saying, <u>Let neither man nor beast, herd nor</u>*

flock, taste any thing: let them not feed, nor drink water:

[8] _But let man and beast be covered with sackcloth, and cry mightily unto God: yea, let them turn every one from his evil way, and from the violence that is in their hands._

[9] _Who can tell if God will turn and repent, and turn away from his fierce anger, that we perish not?_

[10] _And God saw their works, that they turned from their evil way; and God repented of the evil, that he had said that he would do unto them; and he did it not._ (Underline mine)

The Holy Ghost speaks when we fast

If you desire the Holy Spirit to speak to you, fasting combined with other spiritual exercises can trigger it. Pay the price and fast and the Holy Spirit will speak to you in your marriage regarding the concerns you may have.

Acts 13:1-2

[1] _Now there were in the church that was at Antioch certain prophets and teachers; as Barnabas, and Simeon that was called Niger, and Lucius of Cyrene, and Manaen, which had been brought up with Herod the tetrarch, and Saul._

[2] _As they ministered to the Lord, and fasted, the Holy Ghost said, Separate me Barnabas and Saul for_

the work whereunto I have called them. (Underline mine)

The above scripture tells us that as certain ministers of God fasted and ministered to the Lord, the Holy Ghost spoke. This is very good for directions, guidance, and leading. When the Holy Spirit speaks to you expressly, you can never go astray.

Fasting helps to mortify the flesh

Apostle Paul made a list of the works of the flesh as follows in:

Galatians 5:19-21

> [9] *Now the works of the flesh are manifest, which are these; Adultery, fornication, uncleanness, lasciviousness,*
>
> [20] *Idolatry, witchcraft, hatred, variance, emulations, wrath, strife, seditions, heresies,*
>
> [21] *Envyings, murders, drunkenness, revellings, and such like: of the which I tell you before, as I have also told you in time past, that they which do such things shall not inherit the kingdom of God.* (Underline mine)

The above works of the flesh are so dangerous, and they seriously affect a marriage if not properly taken care of through self-discipline, and the power of the Holy Spirit. Some people deceive themselves and refer to them as works of the devil because they want to blame the devil for everything.

Fasting combined with other spiritual exercises is a very effective way of dealing with and mortifying the flesh. Therefore, fast! When couples are in the flesh, they experience all manner of arguments, disagreements, and evil attacks. But fasting will help crucify the flesh and make the couple be filled with the Holy Spirit, and live harmoniously, blissfully, and victoriously in marriage.

Romans 8:9-13

> [9] *But ye are not in the flesh, but in the Spirit, if so be that the Spirit of God dwell in you. Now if any man have not the Spirit of Christ, he is none of his.*

> [10] *And if Christ be in you, the body is dead because of sin; but the Spirit is life because of righteousness.*

> [11] *But if the Spirit of him that raised up Jesus from the dead dwell in you, he that raised up Christ from the dead shall also quicken your mortal bodies by his Spirit that dwelleth in you.*

> [12] *Therefore, brethren, we are debtors, not to the flesh, to live after the flesh.*

> [13] *For if ye live after the flesh, ye shall die: but if ye through the Spirit do mortify the deeds of the body, ye shall live.* (Underline mine)

Galatians 5:16

> *This I say then, Walk in the Spirit, and ye shall not fulfil the lust of the flesh.*

Galatians 5:25

> *If we live in the Spirit, let us also walk in the Spirit.*

Note that it is important for the couple in marriage to live in the Spirit, and also walk in the Spirit.

Medical science research

Medical science studies show that proper fasting has some health benefits of cleansing the body and resetting it.[8]

Take advantage of the benefits of fasting and remain healthy.

Heavenly Father, I ask that you continually fill us with your Holy Spirit as a couple in this marriage. Holy Spirit, we welcome you into our lives, marriage, and every area of our lives. We truly desire intimate fellowship and communion with you all the days of our life in Jesus' name. Amen!

Shaun stood up and started clapping for his wife, as he smiled, and held her and gave her a peck and said, "This is a good message for us. Thanks for the teaching. More wisdom and anointing upon your life. We receive the grace to do the fasting in Jesus' name. Amen!"

Shaun said, "Sweetheart, can I ask a question?"

Mary replied, "Please go ahead and ask your question darling."

QUESTION

Shaun asked, "Sweetheart, should a couple abstain from having sex during fasting periods, especially long fasting like corporate church fasting of 7, 14, or 21 days fasting?"

ANSWER

Mary answered, "That's a very good question. The Bible says in:

1 Corinthians 7:5

> <u>*Defraud ye not*</u> *one the other,* <u>*except*</u> *it be with* <u>*consent for a time*</u>*, that ye may give yourselves to* <u>*fasting and prayer*</u>*; and come together again, that Satan tempt you not for your incontinency.* (Underline mine)

Based on the above scripture, the only time a couple should abstain from sex is during fasting and prayer and that should also be with consent. Consent means husband and wife must agree to it. If one party wants sex, this same scripture says you should not defraud or deny them, because they also have the right to your body as both of you are one flesh. I want to round up my answer to this question by saying that whatever we do, including fasting and prayer, is worth doing well with all seriousness in order to also get excellent results. Also, marry a spiritually mature person who will attach great importance and value to fasting and prayers. In conclusion, I would say abstain from sex during fasting and prayer, as the above scripture says. Any couple who decides to have sex during fasting and prayer is not complying with the above biblical principle and should not also be disappointed or complain that their prayer is not answered. The choice is yours. As for me and my husband, we are not going to have sex during fasting, even if it is for 21 days. No sex for 21 days will not kill us. After all, we were in courtship for one year without sex. What do you say to that? Couples need to grow up spiritually to mortify the flesh by fasting."

Shaun replied, "Thanks darling, for that brilliant wise answer. I totally agree with your answer."

With this, they have come to the end of their morning devotion. They started getting ready for the gym activities. They got ready and left their suite, holding hands and chatting together. They got to the gym, and a young handsome man approached them, and said, "Kalimera," which means, "Good morning."

And they replied "Kalimera."

The young man said, "Please go in and use the gym facilities."

They replied, "Efcharisto." This means "Thank you," in Greek.

The young man said, "Parakalo," which means "You are welcome."

The Perfecto 5-star hotel gym is big, clean, and has different sections. They spent a few minutes going round to see the location of various training machines and equipment. They were satisfied with what they saw. They went straight to the treadmills next to each other, programmed it for 30 minutes. They started with walking and then increased the speed to jog moderately. This is a good cardiovascular exercise that helps with the circulation of blood to and from the heart, and it keeps you fit and healthy. As they did this, *Hillsong worship gospel songs* playlist was on, starting with the track *What a Beautiful Name*. They moved on to the Recumbent Exercise Bike, then the Rowing Machine, and they ended their exercise for the day at exactly one hour.

They got back to their suite, put on their *Hillsong worship gospel songs* playlist, starting with the track *Jesus I Need You.*

They quickly got into the bathroom, cleaned up, and had their shower. They came out refreshed, dressed up, and ready for the Museum Archaeological center, and church tour. They already have pre-booked tickets. It's exactly 11am and their private tour guide knocks on the door.

They opened the door and he said, "Good morning. My name is Aristarchos, and I am your private tour guide for the day to the Museum Archaeological center, and church arranged by Perfecto 5-star hotel."

They replied, "Good morning. Thank you for coming."

They all made their way down to the *Rolls-Royce Phantom 8* and Aristarchos opened the doors for them.

As they got into the car, Aristarchos said, "This is Thera, Thira, or Fira, the capital town of the Island of Santorini, Greece. We have a good museum, and a church we can visit today. This will give you the opportunity to learn some things about the history, traditions, customs, and culture of Greece." He now asked, "Is there any specific thing you would like to find out about the museum, and the church?"

Mr McGregor answered, "There is nothing in particular. Just take us to the Museum, and the church and any other place of interest to tourists, and speak to us as we go along. If we have any questions, we will ask."

Aristarchos said, "That's fine. In that case, we will first visit:

The Museum of Prehistoric Thera, in Fira, Island of Santorini, Greece"

Aristarchos continued, saying, "The Museum of Prehistoric Thera, in Fira, on the Island of Santorini, Greece, is located on the main road in Fira, and this is about 120 metres from the main square. It was built on the site of the former Ypapanti Church which was destroyed in the 1956 Amorgos earthquake.

This well-organized museum gives Santorini's rich history and ancient civilizations. They have on display art and artefacts from the archaeological excavations of the ancient village of Akrotiri, a Cyladic Bronze Age settlement, as well as the ancient settlement of Potamos in south Crete.

The earliest excavations on Santorini Island were conducted by French geologist F. Fouque in 1867, after some local people found old artefacts at a quarry. Later, in 1895-1900, the digs by German archaeologist Baron Friedrich Hiller Von Gaertringen revealed the ruins of ancient Thera on Mesa Vouno. A little later, R. Zahn also excavated in the area of Potamos.

The exhibition is laid out on one floor in the following areas: Geological ancient Thera (Fira), Santorini's history from the late Neolithic period (early 17th century), the peak of Akrotiri society in the 17th century, and aspects of Akrotiri society that include the colony's emerging bureaucratic system, the organization of architecture and city planning as an urban center, the rich and diverse pottery repertoire, the influences of vase and wall painting, elegant jewelry worn by the citizens, and the city and islands' complex network of contacts outside Akrotiri and the Island.

The collections are displayed chronologically, and include ceramics, sculptures, jewelry, wall paintings, and ritual objects. The monumental art of wall-painting is represented in great detail. The Island's network of contacts with the outside world is also explained."[9-10]

After giving them this valuable information and an introduction about the museum, Mr and Mrs McGregor said, "Thank you very much. We are pleased to have you here as our tour guide."

They got into the museum, and were shown around to see all the things Arsitarchos said. Very fascinating, and educational items were on display to tell the story of Santorini Island, Greece. It's really worth being here as a Christian because the New Testament of the Bible was originally written in Greek, and some parts of the Bible were set in places like Athens, and Thessaloniki, Greece. The great Apostle Paul even wrote two epistles, 1st and 2nd Thessalonians, to the church in Thessalonica. This visit provides an opportunity to have an idea of what ancient Greek culture, traditions, and customs used to be like. They left the museum and went to:

St. John the Baptist Cathedral, Fira, Santorini

Aristarchos said this about the church: "This church is a parish of the Catholic Church in Fira, on the Island of Santorini, Greece. It serves as the cathedral of the Diocese of Santorini. The cathedral is located in the city center, in the Catholic neighborhood, near the upper cable car station.

The current church is a baroque structure of blue-gray and cream, and was built in 1823. This cathedral was originally built by the Jesuits of the Apostolic Order. They were missionaries whose task was to spread Catholicism on the Island. Interestingly, Santorini lay on the route of the Crusades. It was completely restored and rebuilt in 1970, after the 1956 earthquake.

The building has a tall bell tower, and this also serves as a clock tower. Inside the church, are displayed portraits of saints and the blessed hung on the pillars.

The church (as one of the few) is open to the public practically all the time. Mass for tourists is held every Sunday at 10 am."[11-12]

They got into the church and moved around this beautiful amazing church, and they also admired the picture artworks displayed, and other features portraying the Christian faith. With feeling of satisfaction, they left the church with the arrangement that Aristarchos will bring them to church for Sunday 10 am morning mass, which is New Year's Day.

When they arrived back to their Perfecto 5-star hotel suite, they decided to pray again since they were fasting. They continued in their prayer till it was time for them to break their fast at 6 pm. They walked down to the restaurant and served their dinner from the buffet. They enjoyed the meal and left to their suite.

They sat next to each other on the sofa chair in the living room to relax.

Mary said, "Honey, thank you for arranging today's tour."

And Shaun replied, "You are welcome darling."

Mary put on the television, and tuned to the *Christian Broadcasting Network (CBN)* and they began to listen to CBN News. After that, they changed to *CBN's 700 Club* featuring *Evangelist Pat Robertson*, and they were encouraged with the testimonies of some Christians.

After a while, they put on their nightwear and went to bed, kissed and said goodnight and slept.

CHAPTER FIVE

DAY 5 – THURSDAY
ALL BATTLES IN MARRIAGE AND
LIFE MUST END

Mr and Mrs McGregor got up early in the morning and exchanged greetings. It was a good night's sleep, and they are awake, refreshed, strong and ready for the day's activities. As their custom is, they start their morning devotion by giving thanks, praise, worship, and prayers.

After that, Mr McGregor said, "It is my turn to preach the Word of God today, and my topic is:

All Battles in marriage and life must end

One of the institutions the devil hates and fights most is marriage. That is why, from the beginning, the serpent attacked the first marital union between Adam and Eve, in Genesis chapter 3. Since that time, the devil has caused a lot of damage to marriages, and lives of the people of God, but today, we have to say enough is enough, as we rise up and establish our victory over Satan, because the battle is the Lord's.

What is a battle?

A battle is a fight, conflict, struggle, or clash between two armed forces. It also means a tenacious struggle to achieve or resist something. A battle involves a hostile, fierce, encounter between opposing forces in combat.

Some scriptures that portray battle and warfare situations

Matthew 11:12

> *And from the days of John the Baptist until now the kingdom of heaven suffereth violence, and the violent take it by force.*

The above scripture depicts a picture of how seriously a believer should act when dealing with the works of the enemy. No jokes! Spiritual exercise violence and force through praying in tongues and scriptural declarations. Remember, the weapons of our warfare are not carnal.

Ephesians 6:12

> *For we wrestle not against flesh and blood, but against principalities, against powers, against the rulers of the darkness of this world, against spiritual wickedness in high places.*

The realm of the spirit is vast and full of invisible, intangible entities, which includes the demons, devil, Satan, etc. And these are forces that a believer has to contend with. We have to significantly step up our warfare mentality and consciousness to defeat the wiles of the devil.

Revelation 12:7-9

> [7] *And there was war in heaven: Michael and his angels fought against the dragon; and the dragon fought and his angels,*

> [8] *And prevailed not; neither was their place found any more in heaven.*

> [9] *And the great dragon was cast out, that old serpent, called the Devil, and Satan, which deceiveth the whole world: he was cast out into the earth, and his angels were cast out with him.*

For you to know how fearless the devil is, he engaged in a fight with Archangel Michael in heaven, the throne of the Most High God. Thank God Archangel Michael defeated him and cast him out of heaven into the earth to be homeless, going to and from the whole earth seeking whom to devour. As a born-again Christian, you must resist the devil, and he will flee from you.

We are victorious in Christ Jesus

It is important to note that no matter how bad, or fierce a battle in marriage or life may seem to look like, as a Christian, as children of God, we must always have it in our consciousness that we are victorious in Christ Jesus because our Lord Jesus has already defeated Satan on the cross of Calvary for us. All we have to do is establish our victory in the name of Jesus, our Lord and Savior. We are overcomers, and more than conquerors in Jesus' name.

Colossians 2:14-15

¹⁴ Blotting out the handwriting of ordinances that was against us, which was contrary to us, and took it out of the way, nailing it to his cross;

¹⁵ And having spoiled principalities and powers, he made a shew of them openly, triumphing over them in it.

John 16:33

These things I have spoken unto you, that in me ye might have peace. In the world ye shall have tribulation: but be of good cheer; I have overcome the world.

1 Corinthians 10:13

There hath no temptation taken you but such as is common to man: but God is faithful, who will not suffer you to be tempted above that ye are able; but will with the temptation also make a way to escape, that ye may be able to bear it.

The above scriptures make it clear that Jesus Christ has overcome the world for us, and no matter the temptation or battle we face in life, there will always be a way out.

Isaiah 43:2

When thou passest through the waters, I will be with thee; and through the rivers, they shall not overflow thee: when thou walkest through the fire, thou shalt *not be burned; neither shall the flame kindle upon thee.*

No matter how bad and terrible a situation may appear to be, be encouraged and know that God is always there with you. He is there to save us from drowning in the waters. As we go through the fiery furnace fire, He is also there with us to save us. Jesus appeared in the fire to save Shadrach, Meshach, and Abednego. See Daniel 3.25. He will never leave you nor forsake you.

God says He will fight our battles

1 Samuel 17:47, "...For the battle is the LORD's, ..."

Exodus 14:14

The LORD shall fight for you, and ye shall hold your peace.

Deuteronomy 28:7

The LORD shall cause thine enemies that rise up against thee to be smitten before thy face: they shall come out against thee one way, and flee before thee seven ways.

Isaiah 49:25-26

25 But thus saith the LORD, Even the captives of the mighty shall be taken away, and the prey of the terrible shall be delivered: for I will contend with him that contendeth with thee, and I will save thy children.

²⁶ And I will feed them that oppress thee with their own flesh; and they shall be drunken with their own blood, as with sweet wine: and all flesh shall know that I the LORD am thy Saviour and thy Redeemer, the mighty One of Jacob.

Psalm 34:19

Many are the afflictions of the righteous: but the LORD delivereth him out of them all.

To avoid misunderstanding the above scriptures that God is there to fight our battles, it is important to trust God for this, and also ask Him for directions and guidance regarding whatever you need to do. Draw near to God, and He will draw near to you – James 4:8. Inquire for the leading of the Holy Spirit.

God has already empowered us to confront battles and warfare and win.

Luke 10:19

Behold, I give unto you power to tread on serpents and scorpions, and over all the power of the enemy: and nothing shall by any means hurt you.

Psalm 91:13

Thou shalt tread upon the lion and adder: the young lion and the dragon shalt thou trample under feet.

The above scriptures clearly tell us that a born-again Christian has been given power to crush the works of the enemy. It's down to us to believe this, and exercise this power. We must have it in our consciousness that we have been empowered to be victorious over all battles in marriage and life.

Matthew 16:19

> *And I will give unto thee the keys of the kingdom of heaven: and whatsoever thou shalt bind on earth shall be bound in heaven: and whatsoever thou shalt loose on earth shall be loosed in heaven.*

Mark 16:17

> *And these signs shall follow them that believe; In my name shall they cast out devils; they shall speak with new tongues;*

As a believer, God has already empowered us to be overcomers, more than conquerors, and victorious in Christ Jesus. We must be continually conscious of this fact. We must have faith in the Word of God as highlighted in the above scriptures.

The weapons of our warfare

2 Corinthians 10:3-4

> [3] *For though we walk in the flesh, we do not war after the flesh:*

⁴ (For the weapons of our warfare are not carnal, but mighty through God to the pulling down of strong holds;)

Psalm 144:1

Blessed be the LORD my strength, which teacheth my hands to war, and my fingers to fight:

It is important to note that the weapons of our warfare are not carnal as stated in the above scripture. We are not to go physical as we fight our battles. Focus on spiritual exercises of prayers, praise, and worship. We are to primarily note that the battle is the Lord's, and keep maintaining that victory consciousness knowing that the Lord is fighting all our battles, and that the enemy has been defeated. Therefore, we are victorious in Christ Jesus.

PRAYER POINTS

- Every monitoring spirit against my marriage, my life, and my family, I say die by Holy Ghost fire in Jesus' name. Amen! Pray!
- You demon attacking marriages through quarrels, arguments, and disagreements, I cast you out, and I say die by Holy Ghost fire in Jesus' name. Amen! Pray!
- Any generational curse, evil pattern in my marriage, and family, known or unknown to me, I banish you now, and I set you ablaze to burn to ashes in Jesus' name. Amen! Pray!
- I uproot and destroy by the power in the blood of Jesus any evil covenant entered by my ancestors.

I command them to be canceled and destroyed by Holy Ghost fire in Jesus' name. Amen! Pray!

- No weapon formed against my marriage, life, and family shall prosper, and every tongue that rises up against us in judgment, I condemn right now in Jesus' name. Amen! Pray! See Isaiah 54:17.

- Every arrow of the enemy against my marriage, life, and family, I say back to the sender in Jesus' name. Let their swords pierce through their own hearts and let their bows be broken in Jesus' name. Amen! Pray! See Psalm 37:15.

- I declare that I and my spouse, and my entire family are fully covered with the whole armor of God and the blood of Jesus, therefore no weapon of the enemy can penetrate us. We have a hedge about us, and as the mountains surround Jerusalem, so the Most High God surrounds us henceforth, even for ever, in Jesus' name. Amen! Pray! See Job 1:10, Ephesians 6:11, and Psalm 125:2.

- Anyone setting up evil altars, digging a pit, or preparing gallows, against my marriage, my life, and my family, I release Holy Ghost fire to locate them now and burn to ashes all their evil plans in Jesus' name. Amen! Pray!

- I declare there is no hiding place for all evildoers against my life, marriage, and family in Jesus' name. Holy Ghost fire, locate them in their caves and crevices, and wherever they may be, on the face of this earth and consume them in Jesus' name. Amen! Pray!

- I declare that I and my spouse, and entire family dwell in the secret place of the Most High God. We are under His wings and feathers, and He is our refuge and fortress at all times. Therefore, we are invisible, untouchable, and undefeatable by the devil in Jesus' name. Amen! Pray! See Psalm 91:1-3

- No evil shall befall me, my spouse, and my entire family, and no plague shall come near our dwellings in Jesus' name. Amen! Pray! See Psalm 91:10.
- Thank you, Lord, for giving your angels charge over me, my spouse, and entire family at all times. Thank you for making us overcomers, more than conquerors, and victorious in Christ Jesus in all battles of marriage, and life in Jesus' name. Amen! Pray!

After the teaching and prayers, Mary shouted a very big "Ameeeeeeen!" and said, "Honey, your teaching and prayer points have set me on fire to pray. You are a prayer warrior indeed. Thank you for the teaching. I am truly blessed." She drew close to her husband and wrapped her hands around his neck and kissed him and said, "I love you." Shaun replied, "I love you too."

Mary said, "Honey, can I ask you a question?"

Shaun said, "Of course you can, darling."

QUESTION

Mary asked, "If a couple is facing a challenge like health, or financial challenges, what do you suggest they should do to take care of the problem?"

ANSWER

Shaun cleared his throat and said, "There are so many things one can do to deal with, for example, *health* challenges. However, I will just give a brief guideline to follow.

Prayer of inquiry and direction: Ask God to specifically let you know what the health problem is, and also direct and guide you on how to deal with it.

Diagnosis: Also see a doctor to examine the person, and carry out appropriate tests to establish what exactly is wrong or to know the sickness. Problems are best tackled when the specific problem or sickness is identified, and dealt with rather than generally.

Concordance: Use your concordance to get appropriate health scriptures and begin to make confessions, declarations, and prayers with them.

Spiritual exercise: Do Bible study, meditations, prayers, thanksgiving, praise, worship and fasting.

Sacrifice: Sow a special seed to end the sickness or plague. See 2 Samuel 24:24-25.

Use your anointing oil, blessed water, handkerchief, etc. Abstain from sin and evil. That's it for now."

Mary replied, "Amen! Thank you for that beautiful answer."

That ended the morning devotion, and they got ready and went straight to the gym to workout. They got on the treadmill and started walking.

Mary asked, "How long are we going to do exercise today?"

Shaun replied, "How long do you want?"

She answered, "Maybe an hour?" Shaun replied, "That's fine,"

They did different kinds of exercise, and when they finished they went back to their suite. They undressed and went straight to the bathroom. They had their bath in the Jacuzzi and while they were there, Shaun started praising his wife's body, saying, "Honey, you are very beautiful, and I love your pointed, moderate breasts, and physique. Thank you for agreeing to marry me. I love you."

When she heard that, she became emotional and said, "I love you too. Thank you for the compliment. You make me blush."

They quickly left the bathroom and went straight to the bedroom and continued their romantic actions. The affection is so strong that as they kissed and caressed one another, they started copulation.

As they did this, Shaun started saying, "You are the best thing that ever happened to me. I love you with all my heart. Thank you for agreeing to marry me. You are simply the best. You are fantastic!" As he said all that, she was responding physically by moving her flexible body, igniting more fire that energized Shaun to continue jerking speedily until he ejaculated. They got back into the bathroom and cleaned up. They dressed up and went down to the restaurant to have their breakfast. After their delicious breakfast, they went back to their suite.

Shaun continued with his romantic, loving utterances to his wife by quoting from the Bible in:

Song of Solomon 4:10-12 (The Living Bible)

[10] *How sweet is your love, my darling, my bride. How much better it is than mere wine. The perfume*

of your love is more fragrant than all the richest spices.

[11] Your lips, my dear, are made of honey. Yes, honey and cream are under your tongue, and the scent of your garments is like the scent of the mountains and cedars of Lebanon.

[12] "My darling bride is like a private garden, a spring that no one else can have, a fountain of my own.

As soon as Shaun finished saying the above romantic, loving words to her, she became emotional, jumped on him, and held him so tight, and kissed him, saying, "I love you more than words can express."

Shaun then brought out his *Selmer Paris Series III Alto Saxophone – Jubilee Gold Lacquer* and started playing this beautiful love song he composed especially for her.

Mary my love
You are so beautiful and caring
Yes you are
Yes you are
And I love you more than words can express

From the very day you agreed to marry me
You've taken my whole heart
And no one
I mean no one

Will take your place as my number one
Oh, my dear Mary

I promise to love you forever
This is every day honeymoon
Till death do us part

Mary, I love you
With my whole spirit, soul, and body
Yes I do
Yes I do
Yes I do, oh!

Immediately he finished singing the lyrics, she was moved to tears, and was speechless. He gave her a handkerchief and she started wiping her tears of joy. The music produced by this unique saxophone was impeccable and exciting. Mary felt like she was in paradise, and heaven on earth imagined. Fantastic!

Mrs McGregor put her hands around her husband's neck and kissed him, and said, "I love you, my lord, and my king. Thank you for that beautiful song and for playing that saxophone so skillfully. It touched me deeply in my spirit. You have made me wet again. I have reached orgasm during this honeymoon again and again."

After she said this, she became so flexible in his arms as one without bones in her body ready to slump to the ground, and Shaun held her firmly and lifted her up and she started smiling with her eyes closed. Shaun took her straight to the bedroom, undressed her, and also undressed himself.

Here we go again as this couple started cuddling and kissing, and he started fingering her so much that she climaxed in the stimulation and could not bear shouting out aloud as she sighed, "Yeaaaah! I love you with all my heart. You are simply the best." Shaun proceeded and did a cunnilingus on her and this further broke and tore her apart, so much that she looked drowsy, being enraptured with love. When Shaun realized she may not be able to cope with sex, he left her to relax and recuperate as she now slept. This is an extraordinary honeymoon in paradise indeed!

When she woke up, they got dressed and went to the restaurant and had a luscious dinner. They finished at the restaurant and went into the Perfecto 5-star hotel center just to see what's happening. They ordered a bottle of *Thymiopoulos Xinomavro,* a non-alcoholic Greek red wine.

A woman walked up to Mrs Mary McGregor and said, "I recognize you ma. You prayed for my aunt at the SUTH in London, and she was healed of her sickness."

Mary said, "Thank God for that. Sorry, but I don't recognize you at all because I do many hospital visits praying for many patients and also evangelizing to win souls."

The woman said, "My name is Jessica, and this is my husband, Lucas. We just got married, and we are here for our honeymoon. I was at the hospital the day you prayed for Auntie Kimberley Elliott."

Mary said, "Oh dear, it's nice to meet you and your husband. My name is Mary, and this is my husband, Shaun. We are also here for our honeymoon. So, how is your auntie Kimberley?"

Jessica answered, "She's doing well."

They all shook hands and embraced each other.

Jessica now said, "Sorry, we have to leave because we've been here for a while. Please keep up with the good work you do praying for patients, and evangelizing to win souls."

Mary answered, "Thank you. See you next time."

They opened their wine, and served in two glasses and they both raised their glasses and said, "Cheers! Long life and prosperity." And Shaun said, "Plus a fantastic honeymoon." And she said, "Yes, fantastic honeymoon indeed."

Mary had a sip from the glass of wine and commented, "This wine is really nice."

Shaun replied, "Yes, it is. I like it too."

They carried on chatting and watching the *GOD TV* channel and those playing snooker games. It's fun to be there.

After a while, they left the center and went back to their suite. They changed to their pajamas, prayed, and went to bed, kissed and slept.

Mary woke up late in the night to urinate and afterward she started caressing Shaun and grabbed his penis and started touching it up and down, and he got a full erection and woke up. They continued caressing each other and then took their clothes off and started making love. Great!

CHAPTER SIX

DAY 6 – FRIDAY
DIVINE DIRECTION, GUIDANCE, AND LEADING IN MARRIAGE AND LIFE

Mr and Mrs McGregor got up early in the morning feeling fine, and in excellent health. They greeted one another, and hugged and quickly used the bathroom to brush their teeth and tongues, and got their Bibles, and notebooks out ready for the morning devotion. They started as usual by appreciating and thanking the Most High God for His provisions, and protection, and for the good time they are having on this honeymoon. They prayed in tongues and made scriptural declarations.

Mary said, "I am doing the teaching today and my topic is:

DIVINE DIRECTION, GUIDANCE, AND LEADING IN MARRIAGE, AND LIFE

Divine direction happens when God clearly speaks to us regarding:

What to do
How to do it
When to do it

Where to do it
Who to do it with

And giving other specific details regarding the instructions. The benefit of divine direction and guidance is that it gives us clarity and confidence to act boldly, and there is a guarantee that we can't go astray or fail, because God is leading us as we follow His will for us to accomplish our purpose in life.

God's divine leading will direct a person to whom to marry; and a couple to their divine purpose or assignment, career, ministry, business, location to live, associations, etc.

Prayer of inquiry: thanksgiving, praise, and worship helps to attract the attention of God to reveal divine secrets to us. When God reveals these secrets, it helps a couple to be in the will of God and to live a blessed and fulfilled life.

Matthew 18:19

> *Again I say unto you, That if two of you shall agree on earth as touching any thing that they shall ask, it shall be done for them of my Father which is in heaven.*

The above scripture encourages a couple to agree on things together. This should include prayer of inquiry and agreement.

Abraham engaged with the Lord, negotiating and asking Him again and again if He will destroy the righteous and the wicked in Sodom in Genesis 18:23-33.

Rebekah made a prayer of inquiry in Genesis 25:23 and God revealed to her that two nations were in her womb – Esau and Jacob.

David inquired of the Lord whether to pursue after the Amalekites and recover all – 1 Samuel 30:8. God said, "Yes."

David inquired of the Lord whether to fight the Philistines in 2 Samuel 5:19. God said, "Yes."

God gives divine directions and instructions

Psalm 32:8

> *I will <u>instruct</u> thee and <u>teach</u> thee in the way which thou shalt go: I will <u>guide</u> thee with mine eye.* (Underline mine)

Noah: God instructed him to make an ark with specifications in Genesis 6:14-16.

Moses: God instructed him to make a tabernacle according to the pattern He showed him in Exodus 25:8-9, & 40.

Joseph: The angel of the Lord instructed him in a dream to take Jesus and Mary to Egypt in Matthew 2:13.

As a couple, God can also give you divine instructions on what to do in your marriage, life, and things to do to promote the Kingdom of God.

God gives divine guidance

John 16:13

> *Howbeit when he, the Spirit of truth, is come, he will <u>guide</u> you into all truth: for he shall not speak of himself; but whatsoever he shall hear, that shall he speak: <u>and he will shew you things to come</u>.* (Underline mine)

Psalm 25:9

> *The meek will he <u>guide</u> in judgment: and the meek will he <u>teach</u> his way.* (Underline mine)

Isaiah 58:11

> *And the LORD shall <u>guide</u> thee continually, and satisfy thy soul in drought, and make fat thy bones: and thou shalt be like a watered garden, and like a spring of water, whose waters fail not.* (Underline mine)

The above scriptures confirm that the Lord guides. A couple can also receive divine guidance for their marriage and life.

God gives divine leading

Romans 8:14

> *For as many as are led by the Spirit of God, they are the sons of God.*

Psalm 23:1-3

> [1] *The LORD is my shepherd; I shall not want.*
>
> [2] *He maketh me to lie down in green pastures: he <u>leadeth</u> me beside the still waters.*
>
> [3] *He restoreth my soul: he <u>leadeth</u> me in the paths of righteousness for his name's sake.* (Underline mine)

The above scriptures confirm that the Lord is our shepherd. He led King David. A couple can also receive divine leading for their marriage and life.

Who are you listening to for directions, guidance, and leading?

Whoever or whatever you listen to has the tendency to influence your marriage and life either positively or negatively. Word input determines output. If you always listen to the Word of God, and other godly materials, that will renew your mind and build your faith, because faith comes by hearing, and hearing by the Word of God. See Romans 10:17.

We live in a world of voices - 1 Corinthians 14:10. Therefore, take heed what you hear – Mark 4:24. As a couple, constantly ensure you listen to the Word of God because it will help you hear the voice of God. Note that you can hear the voice of God, your voice, your spouse's voice, demonic voice, the voice of your parents, in-laws, friends, etc. Who and what you are listening to consistently affects your outcomes, and life. Screen and mind the kind of people you listen to, the kind of music you listen to, as well as the kind of things you see. Guard your heart with all diligence. King David said in *Psalm 101:3, "I will set no wicked thing before my eyes..."* Avoid pornography, violent, and demoralizing TV, social media, and movies as a couple.

Eve listened to the serpent and trouble started in her marriage and for humanity – See Genesis 3.

Abraham listened to Sarah's counsel to go into Hagar, her maid, and Ishmael was born. See Genesis 16:1-3

Samson listened to Delilah and that led to his troubles and death. See Judges 16.

Amnon listened to Jonadab, his friend, and he committed incest with his half-sister, Tamar. See 2 Sam 13.

Ahab listened to Jezebel, and Naboth was killed, and God said He will destroy his descendants. See 1 Kings 21:25.

Be careful who you listen to as a couple because it can negatively affect your mindset and thought patterns. See Proverbs 23:7. Who you give your ears and attention to determines your choices and decision-making as a couple. Don't listen to people who give you wrong counsel contrary to the Word of God, the will of God, and the laws of your country. Who you listen to affects your emotions, feelings, and behavior. Women are more affected by what they hear. That's why Eve was easily deceived by the serpent in their marriage. Men are more affected by what they see. Who you listen to affects your lifestyle, and your life outcomes. Listen to God.

What are the ways God gives us divine directions, guidance, and leading?

God gives us divine directions in the following ways:

Peace: When you are faced with a challenge which involves making a choice or decision, and you lose your peace, become restless, and filled with fear, worry, and sadness, that's a clear indication of a red or danger light to stop. Simply don't go any further since you are troubled in your spirit. On the other hand, if you are filled with the peace that passeth all understanding, that is also an indication of green or go on light. As you go, the peace, and joy of the Lord will begin to open the doors for you to triumph.

Psalm 85:8

> *I will hear what God the LORD will speak: for he will speak <u>peace</u> unto his people, and to his saints: but let them not turn again to folly.* (Underline mine)

As a couple, be determined to live together peacefully, avoiding arguments and quarrels, because it will help create an atmosphere of peace for God to speak.

The Word of God: Studying the Bible and meditating on the scriptures is another way of triggering God to speak.

As you read the Bible, you are filled with light and illumination, and this can give you a Rhema word, and revelations. When God speaks through the Bible, you hold on steadfastly to it, knowing that it will not fail.

2 Peter 1:19

> *We have also a more sure word of prophecy; whereunto ye do well that ye take heed, as unto a light that shineth in a dark place, until the day dawn, and the day star arise in your hearts:*

A couple must devote quality time to studying and meditating on the Word of God. This will provide a way for God to speak. The Bible is a medium of communication for you and God. The Bible contains the promises, prophecies, and principles of God for us.

Audible voice of God: God rarely speaks to us audibly. However, we see in the Bible that God spoke to Prophet Samuel audibly in:

1 Samuel 3:10

> *And the LORD came, and stood, and called as at other times, Samuel, Samuel. Then Samuel answered, Speak; for thy servant heareth.*

Isaiah 30:21

> *And thine ears shall hear a word behind thee, saying, This is the way, walk ye in it, when ye turn to the right hand, and when ye turn to the left.*

The above scripture further states that we will hear a word from the Lord. Just desire and be expectant to hear from God as a couple. Jesus said in:

John 10:27

> *My sheep hear my voice, and I know them, and they follow me:*

Dreams: This is one of the ways through which God communicates to us. It happens when we sleep, whether at night or daytime. Just be careful about what you hear and see in dreams, because some dreams may not be from God. The devil sometimes orchestrates some dreams in order to deceive a person, or you could even have a nightmare which is a product of your thoughts or activities. It's also important to have an accurate interpretation of dreams in order to do the right thing. Judge your dream interpretation with the Word of God as a test of accuracy.

Joel 2:28

> *And it shall come to pass afterward, that I will pour out my spirit upon all flesh; and your sons and your daughters shall prophesy, your old men shall dream dreams, your young men shall see visions:*

Job 33:14-16

> [14] *For God speaketh once, yea twice, yet man perceiveth it not.*

15 In a dream, in a vision of the night, when deep sleep falleth upon men, in slumberings upon the bed;

16 Then he openeth the ears of men, and sealeth their instruction,

The above scripture states that God speaks to us in a dream.

Jacob: He had a dream and saw the angels of God in Genesis 28:12.

Joseph: He had two dreams in Genesis 37:6-9.

Pharaoh: He had two dreams in Genesis 41:1-5.

Nebuchadnezzar: He had dreams in Daniel 2:1-3.

For dreams to be relevant, they must be interpreted correctly. Joseph interpreted Pharaoh's dreams and that helped him and Egypt. See Genesis 41:25. Daniel interpreted Nebuchadnezzar's dreams in Babylon. See Daniel 2:24-45. Note that sometimes God can show somebody a dream which concerns another person. Dreams are sometimes the vehicle that are used to transport the word of knowledge and the word of wisdom.

Visions: This happens when you are awake, and you see a picture which could be stationary or moving like a video. Vision can also happen in the night if you are awake, and not sleeping. Just like dreams, God can show a person a vision which actually relates to another person. In Acts 9:10-11, Jesus spoke to Ananias in a vision concerning Paul. In verse 12, Paul also saw in a vision concerning Ananias coming to him. Just like dreams, visions are sometimes the vehicle that is used to transport the word of knowledge, and the word of wisdom. Jesus gave the word of knowledge, and the wisdom in the visions both men saw.

Ezekiel saw a vision in Ezekiel 1:1
Apostle Paul had a vision in Acts 16:9

Trance: This is a situation between a dream and a vision. It is a half-asleep and half-awake situation, and then you see something. Peter fell into a trance in Acts 10:10.

The Holy Spirit interaction: This happens when the Holy Spirit bears witness with our spirit. See Romans 8:14&16. This sort of situation can also lead to a knowing. In John 13:1&3, Jesus *knew* and also had a *knowing* about certain things. Something can suddenly dawn on you and you will know or perceive things by the inspiration of the Holy Spirit.

The Angel of God: God can speak to us by sending an angel to us. For example, in Luke 1:11-20, Angel Gabriel was sent by God to speak to Zacharias about the birth of his son, John. Angel Gabriel also spoke to Mary about the birth of Jesus in Luke 1:26-38. In Judges 13:3, the angel of the Lord also spoke to Manoah's wife about the birth of her son, Samson. In Matthew 2:13-14, an angel of the Lord spoke to Joseph in a dream to flee to Egypt with Mary and Jesus. In Matthew 2:19-20, the angel of the Lord appeared again to Joseph and to him to return back to Israel with Mary and Jesus because Herod was dead.

Inward or outward hearing of the voice of God: The still small voice in 1 kings 19:12 Elijah heard was inward hearing. Samuel heard an outward external voice in 1 Samuel 3:10.

Through divine situations and circumstances: God is always speaking to us in various ways including our environment. In Proverbs 24:30-34, God used the field and vineyard to speak to a person. Verse 32 says, *"Then I saw, and considered it well: I looked upon it, and received instruction."* In Jeremiah 18:1-6, God asked Prophet Jeremiah to go and observe the potter as I speak to you.

When you are in the Spirit, sensitive and alert, God can speak through your TV, radio, and inscription on a van, or billboard.

Prophetic utterances and confirmations: God sometimes uses a prophet, or a pastor, to speak to us. What they say should serve as a confirmation to what you already believe, know, or expect.

Hosea 12:10

> *I have also spoken by the prophets, and I have multiplied visions, and used similitudes, by the ministry of the prophets.*

Some people have the habit of relying so much on a prophet. Be careful because the Bible says in:

1 John 4:1

> *Beloved, believe not every spirit, but try the spirits whether they are of God: because many false prophets are gone out into the world.*

Matthew 7:15

> *Beware of false prophets, which come to you in sheep's clothing, but inwardly they are ravening wolves.*

Note also that God can speak through other people apart from your prophet. For example, the Bible says in Psalm 8:2 and Matthew 21:16 that God speaks through babes. In Numbers 22:28, God opened the mouth of an ass to speak to Balaam.

What do you do to position yourself to be led by God?

God can lead a person to the right person to marry, ministry, career, location etc. God can also lead a couple. However, we need to position ourselves properly in order for God to lead us.

Honor and reverence God: Always honor and fear God and He will reveal His secrets to you.

Psalm 25:14

> *The secret of the LORD is with them that fear him; and he will shew them his covenant.*

Delight yourself in the Lord: Put God first in all you do. Honor and love Him, and He will take pleasure in leading you.

Psalm 37:4

> *Delight thyself also in the LORD; and he shall give thee the desires of thine heart.*

Show the willingness to be led: God can only lead those who are ready to be led. He cannot lead a stiff-necked and rebellious person.

Romans 8:14 - God leads His sons.

Psalm 23:1-3 - God leads His children.

Meekness: This happens when a person is teachable. You are able to make corrections when you are wrong. You do a U-turn when you are heading in the wrong direction. You are also able to learn, unlearn, and relearn things.

Psalm 25:9

> *The meek will he guide in judgment: and the meek will he teach his way.*

Attitude of inquiry: As mentioned before, if you desire to be led by God, ask Him questions, and He will answer you. The Bible says in:

Jeremiah 33:3

> *Call unto me, and I will answer thee, and shew thee great and mighty things, which thou knowest not.*

Matthew 7:7

> *Ask, and it shall be given you; seek, and ye shall find; knock, and it shall be opened unto you:*

Those who ask God receive, and the same will happen for a couple who ask.

You can't hurry God: Some people think that God is too slow, therefore, they simply carry on with their own plans. In order to hear from God, you must be determined to be patient, because God will make all things beautiful at His appointed time, and not yours. See Eccl. 3:11. He that believeth shall not make haste. See Isaiah 28:16.

Studying and meditation of the Word of God: Keep doing this and God will speak a word in due season to you. The voice of God will come out of the Word. That Rhema word and revelations will come forth when you pay attention to the Word of God. See Psalm 29:3, and Proverbs 6:20-23.

Pay attention to your teachers, pastors, and mentors: As you do this with expectation, God can speak through them a word for you. Samuel paid attention to Eli, his master. See 1 Samuel 3:4-10, & Isaiah 30:20-21.

Obedience to previous instructions: God is likely not to say anything new to you if you have not obeyed His previous instructions. Always hearken, heed, and act on the word of the Lord. *Hebrews 4:7 says,*

"...*To day if ye will hear his voice, harden not your hearts.*"

With this, I bring this teaching to a close. My prayer is that the Most High God will continually direct, guide, and lead us in all we do as a couple, and in life in Jesus' name."

When she finished teaching, Mr McGregor stood up smiling, and clapping for his wife, and said, "Ameeeeen! Thank you very much for this very good teaching. I am truly blessed to listen to you preach, darling." And she replied, "You are welcome darling."

Shaun said, "Can I ask a question darling? And she replied, "Of course you can, sweetheart."

QUESTION

What should a couple do or be doing, if they have been asking God for directions, guidance, and leading for a long time, and God has not spoken to them?

ANSWER

Mary replied, "That's a very good question. I will start by saying that some human beings are very impatient. They want whatever they want from God instantly so to say, but we cannot hurry God. He is not our errand boy. The Bible says in:

Psalm 27:14

> <u>Wait</u> on the LORD: be of good courage, and he shall strengthen thine heart: <u>wait</u>, I say, on the LORD. (Underline mine)

Psalm 40:1

> *I waited patiently for the LORD; and he inclined unto me, and heard my cry.* (Underline mine)

As you wait patiently for the Lord, as the above scriptures say, He will hear your cry and help you. Don't be in a hurry. Just ensure that you are not idle as you wait. Engage yourself with spiritual exercises, and do things which are within the area of your purpose and attainment of your ordained assignment and goal. Ensure you don't ever complain. Always maintain an attitude of joy, gladness, and thanksgiving.

2 Peter 3:9

> *The Lord is not slack concerning his promise, as some men count slackness; but is longsuffering to us-ward, not willing that any should perish, but that all should come to repentance.* (Underline mine)

God is not slack as some men think. He only seems slack to men who are impatient, and don't understand that when it appears as if God is not speaking, He is busy working behind the scenes, paving the way for them. Note also that sometimes we are expecting God to speak to us in a particular way, but He is speaking in another way which we are not paying attention to. Be observant and attentive to hear God.

Ecclesiastes 3:11

> *He hath made every thing beautiful in his time: also he hath set the world in their heart, so that no man*

can find out the work that God maketh from the beginning to the end.

God will speak and make all things beautiful at His own appointed time and not ours. Even when it seems that God is silent, He is saying something, but you probably don't understand. Be patient.

Finally, I would suggest you go through my teaching again, and you will find more points to support the answer to this question. God bless you in Jesus' name."

Shaun said, "Amen! Thank you for that beautiful answer. Much appreciated."

With this, they end this very interesting morning devotion. They started undressing to go to the bathroom to take a shower. As soon as they finished in the bathroom, they got dressed and went straight to the restaurant to have their breakfast.

They got back to their suite and brought out their *Chess game.* They both played skillfully today, so much that Shaun couldn't beat Mary easily. Tough game. At one point, Shaun said, "What's going on today? I am surprised how you have improved so much overnight in this chess game."

Mary said, "You're going to see more surprises because I'm really ready to win this game." They both started laughing.

Shaun replies, "Let's see. And he made his next move and that ended the game."

Mary was sad.

Shaun comforted her and said, "It's only a chess game. Cheer up sweetheart. You could be the winner next time." He embraced her and kissed her, and she put up a smile.

They sat on the sofa, and she put on the gospel music by *Ron Kenoly* starting with the track *All Honor*. They started cuddling, touching and kissing one another and, after a while, they went into the bedroom and had a siesta.

They got up in the evening and got dressed and went to the restaurant and had their dinner. They enjoyed their delicious meal and returned to their suite. They put on their TV and tuned into the *Cable News Network (CNN)* channel and started listening to the news.

After a while, they got up, changed into their nightwear, prayed, went to bed, kissed, and slept.

CHAPTER SEVEN

DAY 7 – SATURDAY
HUSBANDS, LOVE YOUR WIVES;
AND WIVES, SUBMIT YOURSELVES
UNTO YOUR OWN HUSBANDS

They woke up feeling strong and healthy and exchanged greetings and as their usual custom, they quickly used the bathroom to wash their teeth and tongues and face, and came to the living room with their Bibles and notebooks ready for their morning devotion. They started by giving thanks, praise, and worship unto God. God has been good to them to see them through from 1st of January until today 31st of December, and they are very grateful to God for His love, mercy, grace, provisions, and protection. They backed all their thanksgiving by praying powerfully in tongues, and making scriptural declarations.

Shaun said, "Today I will be teaching on the subject titled:

HUSBANDS, LOVE YOUR WIVES

What is love?

The Apostle Paul gave us the meaning of love in:

1 Corinthians 13:4-8 (New International Version (NIV)

4 Love is patient, love is kind. It does not envy, it does not boast, it is not proud.

5 It does not dishonor others, it is not self-seeking, it is not easily angered, it keeps no record of wrongs.

6 Love does not delight in evil but rejoices with the truth.

7 It always protects, always trusts, always hopes, always perseveres.

8 Love never fails. But where there are prophecies, they will cease; where there are tongues, they will be stilled; where there is knowledge, it will pass away.

Now that we know what love is, I will proceed further to give more scriptures instructing husbands to love their wives.

Ephesians 5:25

> *Husbands, love your wives, even as Christ also loved the church, and gave himself for it;*

Colossians 3:19

> *Husbands, love your wives, and be not bitter against them.*

The above first scripture specifically instructs husbands to love their wives even as Christ loved the church. This is called *Agape* love or unconditional love, which you express without any condition. This means that your wife does not have to do something before you show her love. The second scripture above also states that husbands should not be bitter against their wives. This also means that you have to pardon and forgive her shortcomings.

Commandment of love: Note also that love is a commandment and a requirement for all Christians to fulfil, as the following scriptures show. Jesus said in:

John 13:34-35

> *34 A new commandment I give unto you, That ye love one another; as I have loved you, that ye also love one another.*
>
> *35 By this shall all men know that ye are my disciples, if ye have love one to another.*

The Apostle Paul wrote in:

Romans 13:8

> *Owe no man any thing, but to love one another: for he that loveth another hath fulfilled the law.*

1 Timothy 1:5

> *Now the end of the commandment is charity out of a pure heart, and of a good conscience, and of faith unfeigned:*

Another word for love is *charity*. The scripture above states that charity should be out of a pure heart, good conscience, and faith unfeigned. This means that a person filled with anger, bitterness, unforgiveness, malice, and a stony heart cannot truly claim to love. Invite and yield to the Holy Spirit to work on your heart to be renewed.

Romans 5:5

> *And hope maketh not ashamed; because the love of God is shed abroad in our hearts by the Holy Ghost which is given unto us.*

True test of love

Jesus said in:

Matthew 5:44

> *But I say unto you, Love your enemies, bless them that curse you, do good to them that hate you, and pray for them which despitefully use you, and persecute you;*

When you grow in love to the point that you are able to love your enemies, that's an indication that you are really growing and maturing in love because there is no fear in love.

1 John 4:18

> *There is no fear in love; but perfect love casteth out fear: because fear hath torment. He that feareth is not made perfect in love.*

Some of the ways a husband has to continually demonstrate love for the wife

- Husbands must first demonstrate they love God by putting God first in all they do. Honor, and reverence God in all things. Always honor God with your 10% tithe. See Leviticus 27:30 & Malachi 3:10. Thank, praise, and worship God always. Ensure you abstain from evil and sin, and live a holy life.

- As a husband, if you love your wife or anything more than God, it becomes *idolatry* and that is a sin. Don't give your wife £1,000.00 with ease, and give a church offering of just £10.00 to God and also refuse to give tithe to God. Or spend 8 hours at work, 4 hours with your wife, but you can't even pray to God for 5 minutes. That's idolatry. Beware because God is a jealous God. *Exodus 34:14 says, "For thou shalt worship no other god: for the LORD, whose name is Jealous, is a jealous God:"* God is by far more jealous than man. Always put God first, and honor Him above all people and things. Jesus said in:

- *Luke 14:26 of (The Living Bible – (TLB)*

- *"Anyone who wants to be my follower must love me far more than he does his own father, mother, wife, children, brothers, or sisters—yes, more than his own life—otherwise he cannot be my disciple."*

- Always do Bible study, praise, and worship with your wife as the priest of the home.

- Keep telling your wife, "I LOVE YOU."

- Keep telling your wife, "You are the most beautiful woman on earth."

- Address your wife properly. Call her my queen, mummy, sweetheart, honey, darling, my love etc.
- Keep providing and protecting your wife.
- Spend time with your wife, and take her out showing romance and love.
- Give her surprise gifts – money, clothes, jewelry, cards, flowers etc.
- Always remain faithful to your wife and don't commit adultery.
- Be a good leader by showing your wife a good example to follow.
- Don't abuse or lie to your wife.
- Don't deny your wife sex.

Read below this beautiful counsel from King Solomon on how a husband has to relate with the wife in:

Ecclesiastes 9:9 (New International Version – (NIV)

> *Enjoy life with your wife, whom you love, all the days of this meaningless life that God has given you under the sun—all your meaningless days. For this is your lot in life and in your toilsome labor under the sun.*

My prayer for all husbands is that they will love their wives joyfully forever in Jesus' name."

After the teaching, Mary started smiling and clapping for her husband and she said, "Honey, thank you very much for this fantastic message. You are the best husband in the world. I can relate very well with this message because you just preached what you do.

Thank you for loving me so much honey." As she said this, tears of joy started flowing down her beautiful cheeks and she held her husband and kissed him, and said, "I love you." And Shaun held her and said, "I love you too darling," and gave her handkerchief to dry her tears.

Mary said, "Honey, can I ask a question?"

And Shaun said, "Of course you can, darling."

QUESTION

Mary asked, "What is the consequence of a husband not loving his wife?"

ANSWER

Shaun said, "That's a very good question. There is a consequence of not loving and honoring your wife and the Apostle Peter put it like this in:

1 Peter 3:7

> <u>Likewise, ye husbands</u>, *dwell with them according to knowledge, <u>giving honour unto the wife</u>, as unto the weaker vessel, and as being heirs together of the grace of life; <u>that your prayers be not hindered</u>.* (Underline mine)

Husbands, ensure that you always love and honor your wife so that your prayers will not be hindered. Disrespect her and your prayers will not go beyond the ceiling of your house. This could effectively lead to stagnation or even retrogression in life. Respect her, and you will experience the open heavens as your prayers will go straight to God in heaven for instant answers and prosperity in Jesus' name."

Mary said, "Amen! Thank you for that beautiful answer."

Shaun now said, "Honey, please teach on the subject:

WIVES, SUBMIT YOURSELVES UNTO YOUR OWN HUSBANDS

Mary cleared her throat and said, "

What is the meaning of submit?

The Merriam-Webster dictionary gives the meaning as, "To yield to governance or authority." To yield also means to surrender, comply, accept, and back down.

The hierarchy and lines of authority

1 Corinthians 11:3

> But I would have you know, that the head of every man is Christ; and the head of the woman is the man; and the head of Christ is God.

Every nation, organization, and company has a head, and every household must also have a head. That's how God, in His wisdom, has designed it to be, because it will enhance orderliness and work well. And the head has authority over the subordinates or those under him. Hebrews 13:17 says the head will give an account of their subordinates. If you are a rebel, he may not be able to do so with joy.

Graphic picture of the above scripture will look like this:

God ------Christ -------Man --------Woman

Compare the above with an organization which looks like this:

Chief Executive ---------Director -------- Manager --------Supervisor

Will a Supervisor be nasty and challenge the authority of the Chief Executive? No way! If he tries nonsense, he will be severely punished or sacked with immediate effect.

In the same vein, wives, submit and show respect unto your own husbands, knowing he is your superior, as shown in the above scripture and therefore above you in the hierarchy and lines of authority. Submit to promote peace and prosperity in the family even if he is a poor man. Don't try to usurp authority from the man because that's rebellion and that can crash the marriage. You can never have two captains in a ship, and your husband is the Captain or head of the ship or the household. Instead of trying to take over control of the ship, make *suggestions* to him as an Assistant Captain in a very polite way to enable him to steer the ship safely in the right direction to the desired destination. Read how the Apostle Paul put it in:

1 Timothy 2:11-14

> [11] *Let the woman learn in silence with all subjection.*

12 But I suffer not a woman to teach, nor to usurp authority over the man, but to be in silence.

13 For Adam was first formed, then Eve.

14 And Adam was not deceived, but the woman being deceived was in the transgression.

Verse 11 above says the women should learn from their husbands as the head and leader in silence with all subjection. See also 1 Corinthians 14:34-35. The husband is to lead, and the wife to follow. You are a help meet to your husband. See Genesis 2:18. One thing you must try to understand is that God in His wisdom originally created man to head and lead the woman. Any attempt to disrupt this arrangement is dysfunctional in a family setup. That's why even when a husband gives up his position to his wife to lead, she will end up messing things. Did Eve not end up messing things for Adam by going to listen to the serpent and carrying out his instructions? See Genesis 3.

Verse 12 above says a woman should not *usurp* authority over a man.

The Merriam-Webster dictionary gives the meaning of **usurp** as, "To seize and hold (office, place, functions, powers, etc.) in possession by force or without right." This is like planning a coup to overthrow your husband. *Queen Vashti's* strategy was to say 'No' to what the king said. That's the strategy some wives use today as well. They will say 'No' to everything their husband says, including 'No' to sex, 'No' to cooking, 'No' to support with the house bills etc. What a strategy to usurp authority! Just make sure you don't use this strategy for a King Ahasuerus, because he will kick you out. And if he is not King Ahasuerus, he may leave the house for you. See Proverbs 21:19.

Don't be a rebellious or stubborn wife because *1 Samuel 15:23 says, "For rebellion is as the sin of witchcraft, and stubbornness is as iniquity and idolatry…"*

When you are rebellious and stubborn to your husband, it is God who ordained him to be your head, you are resisting, and the consequence is damnation.

Romans 13:1-2.

> *¹ Let every soul be subject unto the higher powers. For there is no power but of God: the powers that be are ordained of God.*

> *² Whosoever therefore resisteth the power, resisteth the ordinance of God: and they that resist shall receive to themselves damnation.*

And if Queen Vashti's strategy fails, they will turn to *Potiphar's wife's* strategy and claim that their husband is attempting to rape them.

Delilah didn't care that Samson loved her. See Judges 16:4. She still betrayed Samson and his enemies captured him. This is another strategy some wives use to usurp power from their husband. Do good and not evil to your husband forever. See Proverbs 31:12.

And if that strategy doesn't work, they will start setting up traps, snares, and nets to claim their husband abused them physically. These are all lies framed to usurp authority from your husband. *Ecclesiastes 7:26 says, "And I find more bitter than death the woman, whose heart is snares and nets, and her hands as bands: whoso pleaseth God shall escape from her; but the sinner shall be taken by her."* Be careful not to hurt yourself in the process of setting traps for your husband because she that digs a pit shall fall into it. See Psalms 7:15, and 9:15.

Don't try to be a *Jezebel*. King Ahab was just a figurehead. Queen Jezebel made decisions for the kingdom. She wrote and sealed letters that were used to kill Naboth. See 1 Kings 21. She threatened to kill Prophet Elijah, and he was so scared that he fled from her. See 1 Kings 19. She misused power and that's how wives who usurp power from their husbands behave.

Some wives are deceivers. During courtship, they will pretend to be very humble and polite, but after the wedding they will start showing their stubbornness. A story was told about a certain woman who always made very nice cups of tea for her husband and also cooked for him. However, after the wedding, the husband asked, "Can you please make me a cup of tea darling?" She replied, "Is anything wrong with your hands? Don't you know where the kitchen is? If you don't cook in this house, you will starve." That's it! A new era has come. In Genesis 18:6, Sarah cooked for Abraham and the guests. And Proverbs 31:15 says the virtuous wife cooks for the household.

What some wives need to understand is that a man who truly loves his wife will prefer to eat only her food. But to avoid cooking for their husband, some of them order food from a restaurant for their husband, and this can never be the same as home-cooked food. Some get a maid who will cook and serve their husband while they do absolutely nothing. They do this thinking they are smart, but they are actually creating an opportunity for their husband to start liking their maid, because she is the one who always cooks and serves him, and he may even start sleeping with her. Did Abraham not end up sleeping with Hagar, Sarah's maid? Did Jacob not end up sleeping with Bilhah and Zilpah, his wives', Leah and Rachel, maidservants? Be careful! Don't play a dangerous game that will work against you. Cook and serve your husband with love, joy, and dignity. He is your head, and king.

Verse 13 above tells us Adam was first formed by God and then Eve. See Genesis 2:21-22. Respect the fact that your husband is older than you. *Job 12:12* says, "*With the ancient is wisdom; and in length of days understanding.*" Also respect the fact that your husband paid for your dowry to marry you, and you changed your surname to his surname because you belong to him. Men's surnames are forever the same. No change. You became Mrs because of Mr. Vashti became queen because of King Ahasuerus. Without the King, there will be no Queen.

Verse 14 tells us Eve was deceived by the serpent. See Genesis 3. This is what happens when a wife usurps authority and begins to lead the husband. The devil will deceive her, and she will be in transgression for doing so. Take your rightful place as a follower. It's a beautiful place to be in. Don't be a rebel.

Some women are so disgusted by the fact that the Bible says they have to submit to their own husbands as unto the Lord. One woman calls it women oppression and therefore strongly advocates for women's liberation and empowerment. This woman questioned why the Bible did not say, "*Husbands submit unto your own wives, as unto the Lord.*"? Is this not rebellion to the Word of God?

Another woman also said this, "I don't believe in all this nonsense about wives, submit to your own husbands. I and my husband are *equal* partners. Ephesians 5:21 says we should submit to one another. Therefore, we take things in turn. If I cook today, he will cook the next day. If I clean the dishes today, he will clean the dishes tomorrow. If I hoover today, he will hoover tomorrow. If I do the shopping today, he will do it tomorrow. If I babysit today, he will do it tomorrow. That's it!"

I asked her, "Are you equal with your boss at work? Do you take things in turns with your boss at work? Do you take it in turns with your husband to breastfeed the baby? Do you share the payment of the bills 50/50 with your husband? She didn't answer any of the questions. Why is it that these sorts of women submits to all men except to their own husbands that God commanded them to submit to? They do the right things everywhere except at home with their own husbands. I call it the disease of familiarity because you see his nakedness. You've got to do a U-turn and submit to your husband and be mightily blessed in Jesus' name.

The Bible further makes it clear that the husband shall *rule* over the wife in:

Genesis 3:16

> *Unto the woman he said, I will greatly multiply thy sorrow and thy conception; in sorrow thou shalt bring forth children; <u>and thy desire shall be to thy husband, and he shall **rule** over thee.</u>* (Emphasis mine)

Most translations, including NKJV, AMPC, GWT, ESV, NAS, NIV, NLT, TM etc. all use the word "*rule*" in the above scripture.

The Merriam-Webster dictionary gives the meaning of "*rule*" as, "The exercise of authority or control: DOMINION."

Let's proceed further and look at some scriptures that instruct wives to submit unto their husbands.

Ephesians 5:22-24

> [22] <u>*Wives, submit yourselves unto your own husbands, as unto the Lord*</u>.
>
> [23] <u>*For the husband is the head of the wife*</u>, *even as Christ is the head of the church: and he is the saviour of the body.*
>
> [24] *Therefore as the church is subject unto Christ, so let the wives be to their own husbands <u>in every thing</u>.* (Underline mine)

Colossians 3:18

> *Wives, submit yourselves unto your own husbands, as it is fit in the Lord.*

1 Peter 3:1

> *Likewise, ye wives, be in subjection to your own husbands; that, if any obey not the word, they also may without the word be won by the conversation of the wives;*

The above scriptures specifically instruct wives to submit unto their husbands as unto the Lord Jesus Christ. If you do not submit to your husband in all things as you would do to our Lord Jesus Christ, you are not keeping up to the standard and therefore need to step up.

One very bad thing some wives do is that they submit to other people's husbands, like their pastor, boss at work, lecturer at school etc. minus their own husband whom God commanded them to submit to. Some of them even kneel down to greet their pastor, bow down to greet their boss at work, and lecturer at school. But when they see their husband, they will shout at him, and stick out their fingers rudely at him. Is this not disrespectful, and foolish? It is indeed foolishness to submit and respect another man more than your own husband whom God commanded you as the number one person to submit to.

A lot of women use money and the success of a man as a yardstick to assess whether they will marry him or not, and this also becomes the basis they use to either submit to him or not. If the man has money, they submit and respect him. If his money finishes, they jilt him for another man who has money. That's all nonsense. As a woman, consider working to make your own money and become successful because there is dignity in labor.

Let me emphasize here that you should not marry a man you cannot submit to or respect. If you marry him because he has money to take care of you, that means you submit to his money and not to him and that is not right. Remember, a man can be rich today, and become poor tomorrow. Consider other potential qualities the man has as well.

Note that the subject of submission is a commandment and a requirement for all Christians to fulfil, as the following scriptures show:

Ephesians 5:21

> *Submitting yourselves one to another in the fear of God.*

1 Peter 5:5

> *Likewise, ye younger, submit yourselves unto the elder. Yea, all of you be subject one to another, and be clothed with humility: for God resisteth the proud, and giveth grace to the humble.*

The above scriptures make it clear that the subject of submission is for all Christians. God resists the proud, but gives grace to the humble. Be a humble wife.

Some of the ways a wife has to continually demonstrate submission to her husband

- Wives must first submit to God and demonstrate they love God by putting Him first in all they do. Honor, submit, and revere God in all things. Always honor God with your 10% tithe – See Leviticus 27:30 & Malachi 3:10. Thank, praise, and worship God always. Ensure you abstain from evil and sin, and live a holy life.

- As a wife, if you love your husband or anything more than God, it becomes *idolatry* and that is a sin. Beware because God is a jealous God. *Exodus 34:14 says, "For thou shalt worship no other god: for the LORD, whose name is Jealous, is a jealous God:"* God is by far more jealous than man. Always put God first, and honor Him above all people and things.

- Always do Bible study, praise, and worship with your husband at home.

- Keep telling your husband, "You are the best husband in the world."

- Address your husband properly. Call him my lord, my king, daddy, sweetheart, honey, darling, my love, etc. Remember Sarah called Abraham, "My lord" in 1 Peter 3:6. Don't call him Tony, or John, or say, "Hey, my guy, dude, or baby, come here." He is not your errand boy. Show respect. Remember, what you call a person or thing is what it turns out to be.

- Obey his instructions, especially if they are not evil, illegal, sinful, harmful, or against biblical principles.

- If you do not say "No" to Jesus, don't say "No" to your husband. See Ephesians 5:22-24 again.

- Be a Proverbs 31:10-31 woman to your husband.

- Always wear decent clothes that will cover your body properly. You are a married woman and not a harlot. See Proverbs 7:10-11.

- Always remain faithful to your husband and don't commit adultery.

- Be a good follower by following your husband's good examples.
- Don't abuse or lie to your husband.
- Don't deny your husband sex.

Read below this beautiful counsel Apostle Paul gave to wives on how to submit to their husbands in:

Ephesians 5:33 (Amplified Bible Classic Edition – (AMPC)

> *However, let each man of you [without exception] love his wife as [being in a sense] his very own self; and let the wife see that she respects and reverences her husband [that she notices him, regards him, honors him, prefers him, venerates, and esteems him; and that she defers to him, praises him, and loves and admires him exceedingly].*

My prayer for all wives is that they will submit to their husbands in everything respectfully forever in Jesus' name."

After the teaching, Shaun started smiling and clapping for his wife and he said, "Honey, thank you very much for this wonderful teaching. This is woman-to-woman talk. I admire your boldness to teach the truth, supporting your teaching with appropriate scriptures. Thank you for being a submissive, gentle, loving, and caring wife. You have just preached what you do. You are precious to me, honey." Shaun held his wife and kissed her, and said, "I love you." And Mary replied, "I love you too, darling,"

Shaun said, "Honey, can I ask a question?"

And Mary said, "Of course you can, darling."

QUESTION

Shaun asked, "What are the repercussions of a wife not submitting to her husband?"

ANSWER

Mary said, "That's a very good question. There is a very serious repercussion of not submitting and honoring your husband. In the case of King Ahasuerus, he had a dual authority as husband and king over Queen Vashti. Queen Vashti lost her crown as a queen, and ceased to be the wife of King Ahasuerus, and was also banished from the palace. The king requested that the queen should be brought to meet his guests but she refused. This is how the Bible recorded it in:

Esther 1:11-12

> [11] *To bring Vashti the queen before the king with the crown royal, to shew the people and the princes her beauty: for she was fair to look on.*

> [12] *But the queen Vashti refused to come at the king's commandment by his chamberlains: therefore was the king very wroth, and his anger burned in him.*

This was a very simple request the King made, but Queen Vashti refused. This request was not criminal, evil, illegal, harmful, sinful, or against biblical principles. Yet she declined to come. Is this not pride, and total disrespect? Looking critically at this case scenario, for Queen Vashti not to submit to King Ahasuerus, a very wealthy and powerful man in charge of 127 provinces, I realized that

Queen Vashti probably did not submit because of pride, indiscipline, and intention to usurp authority from King Ahasuerus, but that landed her in total disaster. She lost everything! Is this not pride, foolishness, and greed?

The king made a decree thus:

Esther 1:20

> *And when the king's decree which he shall make shall be published throughout all his empire, (for it is great,) all the wives shall give to their husbands honour, both to great and small.* (Underline mine)

The above decree says, "*...all the wives shall give to their husbands honour, both to great and small.*" According to this decree, all wives must submit, honor, and respect their husbands whether they are poor like Lazarus, or short like Zacchaeus.

A young beautiful virgin, Queen Esther, was chosen by King Ahasuerus to replace Queen Vashti. There will always be a better replacement for the stubborn wife. Is it not amazing that Queen Vashti did not even commit adultery, yet she lost her husband, and crown as a queen? This goes to show the seriousness of the matter of a wife not being submissive in marriage, and is a lesson for the rebellious wives. Is this not the current trend in marriages where some wives rebel against their husbands even on very trivial matters, like come and meet my guests, and they will refuse just like Queen Vashti, and the marriage will crash? Even if you are the President, Prime Minister, Governor, Company Chief Executive, or Director, do all that at work. When you get home, submit to your husband because that's his domain as your lord and king. Respect him, and don't deny him food and sex. My prayer is that God will grant all wives the grace to submit and surrender to their husbands in everything as unto our Lord Jesus, in Jesus' name."

Shaun said, "Amen! Thank you for that wonderful answer darling."

This effectively brought to a close today's morning devotion. They immediately started undressing and went into the bathroom to take a bath. He started washing her body and commented, "Your body is so smooth and attractive, and I desire to devour you." She replied, "Go on then. I belong to you sweetheart. I'm at your beck and call, my love."

Shaun said, "Thank you my queen. Your wish is also my command. Anything you want, I will give it to you, up to half of my kingdom darling. You are my better half." They both started laughing. With this sort of welcoming response from her, Shaun immediately had a firm erection ready for action. As soon as they finished their bath, they started cuddling and kissing and Shaun penetrated her and started making love to her. Fantastic! They finished making love and got dressed and went straight to the Perfecto 5-star hotel restaurant to have their breakfast.

While they were having their scrumptious meal, he asked her, "I hope you are having a good time on this honeymoon?" She replied, "Of course I am. I am very proud of you honey, and I love you very much. Thank you for all your love, support, and care." As she said this, tears of joy started rolling down her beautiful face and Shawn wiped the tears with her handkerchief and gave her some fresh mango juice to drink. He robbed her back gently and gave her a peck and she said, "Thank you sweetie." After a while, they left the restaurant back to their suite.

As they got back to their suite, she got out all their dirty clothes and contacted the Perfecto 5-star laundry services department to come and take them. This only takes a few hours to be ready.

They now got ready to go to the salon right there at the Perfecto 5-star hotel premises. They want to do their hair, manicure, pedicure etc. because tomorrow is Sunday, and also New Year's Day, and they have to look good. As they got there, they met with the proprietress, Lydia. She is a beautiful lady, and full of smiles. She immediately welcomed them into her well-equipped, and well-staffed salon, saying, "Good morning. Please sit down and make yourself comfortable."

They said, "Good morning, and sat down."

Lydia asked, "How can I help?"

Mrs McGregor replied, "I and my husband are here to do our hair, manicure, and pedicure."

Lydia said, "That's fine. You people came at the right time. We are not very busy now. I will assign my staff to start the work immediately."

Mrs McGregor's husband is a millionaire, so she doesn't bother herself at all with the price list of things like this. They are simply peanuts. However, Shaun is mindful because every penny counts to an astute business millionaire man.

Lydia gave them malt drinks, assorted chocolates, and biscuits. They said, "Thank you very much."

As they fixed their hair, gospel music songs by *Michael W. Smith* were playing in the background, starting with the track *Above all*. They finished doing all their salon stuff and left back to their suite.

When they got back to the suite, Shaun looked at his wife with great affection and said, "Honey, you are very beautiful. I love your new hairstyle, manicure, and other make-up. I love you." He held her and gave her a kiss.

Shaun said again, "Can you do a catwalk for me stylishly like a supermodel in this outfit and new hairstyle?"

Mary said, "Yes oh, I will, my lord, and my king." She walked around stylishly in the sitting room showing off her great feminine physique. Shaun admired his wife exceedingly, became elated and said, "You are the most beautiful woman in the world. Thank you for agreeing to marry me. I admire and adore you, my love."

When Mary heard this, she became emotional and started blushing with deep affection and moved to tears. Shaun wiped her tears with a handkerchief and held her close to his arms, and they started kissing, and he said, "I love you." And she replied, "I love you too."

They sat down on the sofa next to each other and turned on the TV to the sports channel to watch the English Football league. *Manchester United* versus *Chelsea* playing. The game has just started.

Shaun is a Manchester United fan. He asked his wife, "Honey, which club do you support?" She replied, "Manchester United, of course. My husband's club is my club, and what he loves is what I love." Some families are known to get into arguments, quarrels, and even fights because they support different clubs. Mr and Mrs McGregor support the same club and this will help promote togetherness and oneness in marriage. No divisions.

As they were seated in the sitting room, they heard a knock on the door and Shaun opened, and it was the laundry attendant with their clothes. Shaun collected the clothes and thanked him.

Shaun put the clothes in the wardrobe and reminded his wife to get her clothes and other stuff ready for tomorrow's 10 am Sunday service. They will be at the St. John the Baptist Cathedral, Fira, Santorini for the 10am service, and they must be ready by 9.30am because Aristarchos is coming to pick them up, to the church.

While they watched TV, Shaun said, "I just want to let you know I've got tickets for us to be on the Island of Naxos, Greece next Monday by God's grace. We will travel to the nearby Island of Naxos by ferry. That will give us the opportunity to go sightseeing of more of the Greek Islands, see the work of nature, and breathe in fresh air. I hope that's fine darling?"

Mary said, "Certainly, yes darling. I have not been on a ferry before, so I'm looking forward to that adventure."

Shaun said, "That's great."

Mary turned to her husband and said, "Honey, I am hungry. Can we go to the restaurant and have something to eat?" Shaun said, "Yes my love. Let's go." They had their scrumptious meal and returned to their suite to relax and later got up for their New Year's Day midnight prayers.

After relaxing for a while, they both went into the bedroom and slept off to wake up before midnight for their New Year prayers.

They woke up at 11.40 pm and washed their teeth and tongues and started chatting about the things God did for them as they look forward to the New Year in a few minutes.

CHAPTER EIGHT

DAY 8 – SUNDAY
THE END OF AN ERA; AND
A NEW ERA

It's exactly 0.00 am and Mr and Mrs McGregor shouted aloud, "Happy New Year" to one another and said, "Congratulations! We made it into the New Year." They held one another firmly and started kissing with their eyes closed while they also felt the warmth emanating from their affectionate closeness. They are full of joy and excitement that they are alive to see and to enjoy the New Year.

They started thanking, praising, and worshiping God for all the great and mighty things He did for them the last year, especially for excellent health, prosperity, and their marriage. They made scriptural declarations of the things they expect and desire for the New Year. They prayed in tongues powerfully.

Shaun said, "Honey, we are not going to fast today. Let's take a day off today and celebrate our New Year by having fun. I hope that's fine with you?"

Mary said, "That's fine."

Shaun continued, "Honey, please do the teaching today."

Mary replied, "That's alright. My topic for today is:

THE END OF AN ERA; AND A NEW ERA

What is an era?

The Merriam-Webster dictionary gives the meaning as, "A fixed point in time from which a series of years is reckoned; A memorable or important date or event; especially one that begins a new period in the history of a person or thing."

An era simply means a period of time characterized by events and history. For example,

Today marks the end of last year's era, and the beginning of a New Year era.

Last Sunday, Christmas Day marked the end of us being single, and the beginning of a new era of married life. (I will focus more on this area)

When you graduate from school, it marks the end of an era, and when you get work employment, that's the beginning of a new era.

When there is a change of government after four years; that marks the end of an era, and the beginning of a new political era.

When you move from one city to another, that's end of an era, and beginning of a new era.

When you move home, that's end of an era, and beginning of a new era.

When you give your life to Jesus and receive salvation, that's the end of an era of unbelievers, and the beginning of the born-again Christian era.

Born-again Christian

2 Corinthians 5:17

> *Therefore if any man be in Christ, he is a new creature: old things are passed away; behold, all things are become new.*

You must be a born-again Christian as a couple to enjoy the benefits of the above scripture in Christ Jesus. Once a person receives salvation that marks the end of the unbeliever era, and the beginning of a new era to live life like a heavenly kingdom person. Old things, old eras have passed away, behold all things, new era have become new. Your attitude and lifestyle must change as a believer in Christ Jesus.

There will always be a distinction between the old and new era. And to have a better new era, couples and individuals must make a deliberate plan for the present and future.

PREPARE TO BE MIGHTY IN THE NEW ERA

Nothing just happens. Always prepare for the new era. As a couple, prepare for the marriage journey in order to have a successful blissful marriage. Don't leave it to chance.

2 Chronicles 27:6

> *So Jotham became mighty, because he prepared his ways before the LORD his God.*

A lot of people desire to be mighty in life and that is good indeed. But to be mighty does not just happen.

Preparation comes before you become mighty. For example, when you prepare for an examination, you will pass. When you prepare for a sports event, you will win. When you prepare for your business, you will make a profit and prosper. The above scripture tells of the secret of Jotham's success. Preparation! Bearing this in mind, we ought not to dabble into matters, especially marriage, without adequate preparations. In order to excel in whatever we do, we must endeavor to prepare well.

Preparations will:

- Make you pray, fast, and rely on God.
- Make you research further.
- Make you make inquiries about what you are about to do.
- Make you pay attention to details.
- Reveal to you unexpected things you need to know and do.
- Make you confident.

Preparation will make you successful. Quit cutting corners, scheming, and seeking a quick fix. Ensure you apply biblical principles in all you do, even though the standard is high, because it is for your own good. The beauty of applying biblical principles in all you do is that after a while, you will become used to it, and you will be mightily blessed for being obedient to the Word of God. To be the best in any field, you must be fully prepared. For example, to win an Olympic medal takes very serious preparations. The same goes for people who win awards for different things. You achieve such success through meaningful preparations. And it's important to mention here that having a good teacher, coach, or mentor will help your preparations. It may cost you money to hire somebody to help you prepare, but when you achieve your desired success you will also see that it is worth it.

Preparations for the new era in marriage

It's important to make preparations in the following areas in order to have a blissful and successful marriage.

Spiritual and personal development goals: The couple needs to continually do Bible study, meditations, thanksgiving, praise, praise, worship, fasting, and be dedicated members of a church. They must also be committed to reading good Christian instructional books, attending seminars, workshops, and conferences to keep updating themselves.

Family goals: Appropriate preparations have to be made by the couple regarding the intended size of family, contraceptives to use, etc.

Health goals: The couple should prepare to eat the right balanced nutritious food, proper exercise, and do regular appropriate medical check-ups.

Financial goals: The couple must trust God to be their source of financial provision, and therefore, also honor God consistently with their tithes and offerings. The couple should make plans on how to make financial investments, and possible business set up if needed.

Career goals: The couple also have to discuss future career changes if needed.

The above preparations are just a simple guide. They should be discussed, and developed further by the couple, and this is subject to reviews from time to time. Ensure that these plans are written down.

Behold, I do a new thing in a new era of marriage and life

Isaiah 43:19

> *Behold, I will do a new thing; now it shall spring forth; shall ye not know it? I will even make a way in the wilderness, and rivers in the desert.*

God says in the above scripture, "*Behold, I will do a new thing;..*" in this new era of our marriage and life. My husband and I are a living *testimony* that God is true to His Word. Just last Sunday, Christmas Day, our wedding day, and first day of our new era of marriage and honeymoon, God showed up and gave me and my husband the miracle of penis enlargement. We are euphoric about this miracle, and we know this is just the beginning. Thank you, Lord Jesus.

Keep on seeking God in the new era of marriage and life

2 Chronicles 26:5

> *And he sought God in the days of Zechariah, who had understanding in the visions of God: and as*

long as he sought the LORD, God made him to prosper.

The above scripture tells us that King Uzziah sought the LORD, and as long as he did that, God made him to prosper. This clearly tells us that continuous consistent seeking of the LORD is the secret to prosperity and success in marriage and life.

My prayer is that the Lord will mightily bless and prosper everyone in the new era of marriage and life in Jesus' mighty name."

This brings to an end the teaching by Mary. Shaun stood up respectfully, and started smiling and clapping for his wife for the teaching. Shaun said, "Honey, this is a wonderful message you've just preached, and I love it. I am truly blessed. I declare more grace, anointing, and wisdom upon your life in Jesus' name."

Mary affirmed the prayer and said, "Ameeeeen! Thank you very much my lord." They held one another and kissed and went straight to the bedroom. The time now is 2.00 am, and they set their alarm to wake up at 8.00 am to get ready for their 10 am church service. They kissed and slept.

The alarm rang at exactly 8 am, and they exchanged greetings and said, "Happy New Year," to each other again. Mary dressed the bed properly. And they went straight to the bathroom. They washed their teeth and tongues, Shaun shaved, and they had their shower and started getting ready. Mary put on playlist gospel songs by *Cece Winans,* starting with the track, *Mercy Said No.*

Shaun got out his *Giorgio Armani* navy blue suit with strips, *Christian Dior* white shirt and red tie with blue stripes, *Gucci* black belt and shoes to match. He quickly dressed up, combed his hair properly, and sprayed his *Calvin Klein, Eternity for Men* perfume.

Mary brought out her *Charlotte Tilbury Beauty Check-in kit,* and did a fantastic make-up. While she was doing it in the bedroom, Shaun said, "Honey, please keep the make-up moderate. You know you're a very beautiful woman already and I love you. Remember, we are going to church and not to a party."

She said, "Yes, I know all that. I am keeping it moderate. But you know I have to look good for my lord and my king as well, and today is New Year."

After doing her make-up, she went out to the living room and saw her husband ready, and she said, "You are ready already. You look so smart darling, in your outfit, and smart hairstyle. I love you."

Shaun said, "Thank you darling. You know it takes me just a few minutes to get ready. Please go and put on your dress. Aristarchos will soon be here to take us to church."

Mary put on her *Louis Vuitton* elegantly made blue dress with white stripes, and a blue hat to match. She put on her *Dolce & Gabbana* shoes, and handbag to match. She also put on her complete set of *Yves Saint Laurent* bracelet, necklace, wristwatch, and earrings to match. She put on her *Louis Vuitton symphony perfume* to smell good. She looked in the mirror and was satisfied. She called out to her husband, "Sweetheart, I am ready."

Shaun joined her in the bedroom and said, "You are looking stunningly beautiful and gorgeous darling. You smell good too."

Mary replied, "Thank you."

Shaun held his wife and kissed her, and said, "You are so sweet, and I love you." And Mary said, "Thank you very much."

It's exactly 9.30 am and they heard the doorbell. He opened the door, and it was Aristarchos, and he said, "Kalimera kyrie," which means, "Good morning sir."

He said again, "Kali chronia," which means, "Happy New Year."

Mr and Mrs McGregor replied, "Kali chronia."

They went down to the *Rolls-Royce Phantom 8* car and Aristarchos opened the doors for them, and drove them to *St. John the Baptist Cathedral, Fira, Santorini* for the 10 am service.

When they got there, they alighted and Aristarchos told them he would be back after the service to bring them back to Perfecto 5-star hotel.

As soon as they got into the church, they were greeted by the ushers, "Kali chronia" and they replied, "Kali chronia." They shook hands and embraced each other with beaming smiles on their faces. The church is beautifully decorated with lights and flowers because of the New Year celebration. The ushers showed them where to sit, and gave them the bulletin which was written in Greek. They went on their knees and prayed briefly, and sat down.

At exactly 10 am, Bishop Alexander Papadopoulos, Reverend Sebastian Tobias, and the mass servants came to the altar from the room connected to it. Everybody stood up, and Bishop Alexander Papadopoulos said, "Kali chronia" to the church, and the congregation responded, "Kali chronia Bishop," and he declared the service open and gave a short prayer for the congregation.

The first reading was taken from 1 Samuel 24:25, and the second reading was taken from Isaiah 43:18-19. The gospel was taken from the book of John 15:1-5.

Bishop Alexander thanked the Lord for the last year, and prayed that this year will be a much better year in all ramifications. He preached that every Christian must learn to trust God in all things, especially in these last days. After his ministration, communion was served, and offerings were collected. The benediction was declared and the service ended.

After the mass, Shaun asked his wife, "Honey, how do you find the service?"

She said, "That's fine. We give God all the glory." They came out of the church and took some pictures with their mobile phones. Aristarchos came back and took them back to Perfecto 5-star hotel, and they went straight to the restaurant to eat. They have already canceled today's fasting because of the New Year.

Mr and Mrs McGregor settled down and had a scrumptious meal. The Greeks have very popular dishes, like Moussaka, Papoutsakia (Stuffed eggplants), Pastitsio (Greek lasagne), Souvlaki (Gyros), Soutzoukakia (Greek meatballs), Seafood, Stifado (Greek beef stew), Tomatokeftedes (Tomato fritters), Spanakopita, Greek salad, Greek potatoes etc.[13]

To celebrate this New Year, they decided to try out some Greek food. They served some Moussaka,

Papoutsakia, Soutzoukakis, and Greek salad. They also got some fresh fruit drinks.

The Greeks have very good wines produced on the Island of Santorini, like Assyrtiko, Athiri, and Aidani.[14] These wines are made from white grapes on the Island. They also have Greek red wines like Papaioannou St George Agiorgitiko, Thymiopoulos Xinomavro, and Kourtaki Mavrodaphne.[15]

Mr and Mrs McGregor are mainly interested in non-alcoholic red wines. So they decided to try *Papaioannou St George Agiorgitiko* Greek non-alcoholic red wine.

The restaurant is in a vibrant state today. A bit busy, with music playing in the background as they enjoyed their meal. Some people were busy singing and dancing in one corner of the restaurant. After their delicious meal, they went back to their suite.

As soon as they got back to their suite and relaxed a bit, Mary said to Shaun, "Honey, can I make some calls to my family and friends now to wish them happy New Year?"

Shaun replied, "Yes, you can, honey. I will do the same thing."

They deliberately turned off their mobile phones to avoid distractions on this honeymoon. Apart from this, Mr and Mrs McGregor are a highly disciplined, mature Christian couple who believe in investing and managing their time properly on things that will benefit them. Time is life and money; therefore they never waste their time all day on frivolous, unproductive social media issues on their mobile phones like most people do. Never! Instead, they will read their Bible, or a book, listen to a preaching or gospel music songs, pray, praise, or worship God. They gospel, not gossip. Social media gossip addicts belong to the riffraff in the society. Be a serious-minded heavenly kingdom citizen as a born-again Christian.

As soon as she turned on her mobile phone, she saw many missed calls, Texts, WhatsApp, Twitter, Facebook, and Instagram messages, but she ignored all of them. Straightaway, Mary called her parents and she got through to Paul and Brenda and said, "Hello Dad, this is Mrs McGregor calling from the Island of Santorini, Greece. Happy New Year to you, Dad and Mum."

Mary's dad put the phone on speaker so that her mum could also hear, and he said, "Whao! Good to hear from you, Mrs McGregor. I like your new surname. Happy New Year to you darling. Your mummy is beside me as I speak to you. How are you enjoying your honeymoon so far?"

Mary replied, "Great! My husband is the best husband in the world. He is so lovely, and great. I am truly blessed to have him as my husband. Dad and Mum, thank you for giving us your blessing to get married."

Brenda came on and said, "Happy New Year Mrs McGregor. We are excited to hear from you. How is your husband?"

Mary replied, "He is right here with me but on the telephone to his family and friends."

Paul said, "Greetings to your husband. Please take good care of yourself and keep in touch regularly. I love you sweetheart."

Mary replied, "Thanks Dad and Mum. Goodbye for now." And they ended the call.

Mary called Mr and Mrs Evans.

Mrs Priscilla Evans, her cousin, picked up the phone and screamed out aloud, saying, "Happy New Year Hotdog. I'm so excited to hear your voice. How is your husband?"

Mary replied, "Happy New Year to you Priscoh. My husband is fine. How is Barry your husband and your baby?"

Priscilla replied, "They are fine. I hope you are enjoying your honeymoon?"

Mary answered, "Yes, I am enjoying the honeymoon. The Island of Santorini is a great place to be."

Priscilla said, "Tell me about it. When I had my honeymoon on the Island of Majorca, Spain with Barry, my husband, we really had a good time. So I believe you are definitely having a fantastic time with your millionaire husband, Shaun." They both started laughing.

And Mary replied, "You this woman, please leave me alone."

Priscilla said, "Please give me a little gist, you pretender." They both started laughing again.

Mary replied, "Shaun is the best husband in the world. He loves me, and I love him too."

Priscilla said, "I know it. Please take good care of him, and yourself. Cheers!" They both ended the call.

Mary called Jane Foster, her former colleague at Elohim Cars, but her line was busy, and she ended the call. Mary now scrolled down through her text messages and replied to a few important messages from people who sent wedding congratulation messages. And she said, "That's it for now."

Meanwhile, Shaun also called his own family, friends, and company staff and replied to some of his text messages as well.

They got together after the calls and Mary took out two glasses and a bottle of *Saint Viviana Cabernet Sauvignon* non-alcoholic red wine and served for two. They both raised their glasses and said, "Cheers! Long life and prosperity. Happy New year, and happy new era in our marriage and life."

Husband and wife meetings

As they sat on the sofa drinking their wine, Shaun said to his wife, "Honey, there is something very important I would like to discuss with you."

Mary said, "I hope it's not something bad?"

Shaun replied, "Oh no! Not at all bad. It's just that I would like us to start something in this new era of our marriage and life which I believe will greatly help to guide us to grow, mature, and have a blissful marriage."

Mary said, "That sounds great. Please tell me about it darling."

"Yes, I will," Shaun replied. He continued, "In line with the message you preached today, I would like us to be having weekly meetings of about one hour. I would like to call it, '*Husband and wife meeting.*' The purpose and agenda of the meeting is to provide us a special forum where we can share and discuss anything whatsoever which will include things like:

- Promotions at work and in business, and successes.
- Any challenging issue that we need to tackle together.

- Any major issues, like career change, and business investments.
- Any health issues, and emotional pain.
- Any trespasses and wrongs done by any of us so that we can apologize straightaway, and forgive rather than carrying grudges about or keeping malice.
- Opportunity to just feel free and talk about just anything bothering our minds. Just open up and talk. If we don't open up and communicate regularly and properly, it will be hard to achieve transparency, oneness, and intimacy.
- We have to keep a summary record of the key things that we discuss so that we can easily make reference to them and verify what and when we discussed the issue, the action we are to take to handle the issue. We are both accountable to one another to ensure we succeed in this marriage. You will be the one to keep the summary record of our discussions. Please note that the things we will discuss in these meetings are also confidential.

When Shaun finished talking, Mary stood up and started clapping for her husband and said, "Excellent! Perfect! This is a very good idea and I support it 100%. As a matter of fact, can we start it today because I even have something very important I have been trying to talk to you about, but I have been looking for the right time and opportunity to discuss it with you?"

Shaun said, "Yes, we can start today and now. Please feel free to discuss it with me now so that we can commence appropriate action."

Mary continued, "Just last night, I had a dream. And in the dream, I found myself preaching in a very big stadium to over 70,000 people and an angel of the Lord was beside me. As I was preaching, a lot of miracles were happening. Blind eyes opened, the lame walking, people getting up from their wheelchairs, and throwing away their clutches, the dumb speaking, deaf ears opened, evil spirits crying out, casting out devils etc. As I just came off the pulpit, you said to me, 'This is a glorious ministration Woman of God. I love you and I will support your ministry as an Evangelist with everything I have.' And then I woke up." The dream looked so real. This is the third time she's had this kind of dream.

When she finished sharing the dream, Shaun said, "That's great! I already know God called you to be an Evangelist and I will support you with everything I have as your husband. I would like to suggest that we pray to God for directions, guidance, and leading on what, when, and how to get this assignment started and done."

Mary said, "My lord, that's a very good suggestion you've just made. Thank you for agreeing to support me."

Shaun now asked her, "What will now happen to your Marketing career and your job as the Marketing manager at the National Bank in London?"

Mary said, "That's just a career, this is my purpose in life, and a call from God. Therefore, this is superior to that job. Besides, I feel more fulfilled doing the work of God. Preaching, helping people, and evangelizing. As I am discussing this whole thing with you now, I feel like a burden is lifted off my shoulders, and I really feel relieved you brought up this discussion."

Mary held her husband and kissed him and said, "Thank you very much darling."

Shaun said, "You are welcome."

The meeting continued, and Shaun said, "As you already know, I have houses in London, Birmingham, and Edinburgh. When we come back from our honeymoon, I would like you to vacate your East Dulwich, London apartment and join me in my Kensington Mansion. Is that ok?"

Mary said, "With all pleasure. I will, my lord."

Shaun now said, "Excellent! Is there anything else you want us to discuss in this meeting?"

She said, "No." Shaun replied, "Please do a brief summary of our discussion today for reference and reminder purposes. We will be having this '*Husband and wife meeting*' every Friday evening from 7pm to 8pm. Is that ok?"

Mary said, "Yes. That's perfectly fine with me." With this they ended the '*Husband and wife meeting*' for the day.

As they sat on the sofa in the sitting room, they put on the television and tuned in to *Trinity Broadcasting Network (TBN)*, and *Evangelist Joyce Meyer* was preaching. Immediately Mary saw her, she said, "That's my mentor preaching." Mary had read most of her books, listened to many of her preaching, and she was following in her footsteps. Evangelist Joyce Meyer is preaching on the subject: Battlefield of the mind.

When they finished listening to her teaching, they got dressed and went to the restaurant to have their dinner.

After their luscious meal, they came back to their suite, sat in front of the TV, tuned in again to *TBN*, and this time, it was *Bishop T D Jakes* preaching on the subject of faith.

They finished listening to this message, had a shower, and changed into their nightwear, and sprayed a bit of their perfumes. They prayed and acknowledged that it was a great way of spending the first day of the year together. Shaun reminded her they will be on the Island of Naxos tomorrow, and they have to be ready for the chauffeur Aristarchos to pick them up at 7 am to be at the Athinios port, their port of departure. They've got tickets for the journey. They got under the quilt, kissed, and said, 'goodnight' to each other, and slept.

CHAPTER NINE

DAY 9 – MONDAY
TRIP TO ISLAND OF NAXOS, GREECE

They woke up feeling very strong and well. They exchanged greetings pleasantly and asked, "How was your night?" They both responded, "Fine." They brushed their teeth and tongues in the bathroom, and went out to do their morning devotion.

They started by giving thanks, praise, and worship unto the Lord. They prayed and committed their Island of Naxos trip tour into the hands of God to and fro. They canceled their Bible study and teaching for this morning because of the ferry trip to the Island of Naxos. They decided to do it later when they come back from their trip.

They quickly got into the bathroom, had their shower, and got dressed, and got ready for the ferry trip.

Aristarchos came at exactly 7.00 am and took them straight to Athinios port. He gave the following information, saying, "The Island of Naxos, Greece is bigger than Santorini. The capital town is Chora. The Island of Naxos has a variety of attractions which includes historical sites, beaches, hotels, and villages.[16]

The journey time by ferry is about 1 hour 40 minutes to 2 hours. The following ferry company operators ply the route: Blue Star Ferries, Seajets, Minoan Lines, and Saos Anes.[17] Some of them go direct, and some stop at different ports from Santorini to Naxos."

Mr and Mrs McGregor have booked tickets to follow the Unique Ferry operators known for their excellent safety record and services. They boarded the ferry and Mary said to Shaun, "This is beautiful and lovely. This is my first time on a ferry." Shaun said, "I'm glad you like it."

They were taken around a few sections of the ferry and given some information about Health and Safety measures. They sat down watching the quiet sea waters, rocks, ships, ferries, and the bright blue-white sky. They inhale the fresh air as they come out to stay in the balcony area for a better view of the work of nature. Great!

They made their way to the dining area where they had a buffet prepared with a wide range of Greek food, and other continental dishes. They served English breakfast, with tea, orange, and mango juice, and water. As they finished their meal, they realized they would be in Naxos in just about 10 minutes.

As they got off the ferry, they looked around and saw the beautiful beach and the chauffeur, Apollos, arranged to pick them up, was already there with a placard inscription, "Mr and Mrs McGregor." They saw Apollos, and approached him and exchanged greetings. They got into his *Range Rover Luxury SUV,* and he drove off heading for the:

The Archaeological Museum of Island of Naxos

Apollos said, "The Archaeological Museum of Naxos, Greece is a historical monument located in a Venetian building, built between 1600 and 1800 for the Jesuit school established in 1700, later becoming the Archaeological Museum in 1972.

The museum houses collections from the Early Cycladic period, including the famous marble figurines from Naxos, Kato Kouphonisi, Keros, and from the Late Mycenaean period, which includes stirrup jars and other grave goods from chamber tombs and other graves from the Kamini mound and Aplomata. A smaller area is given over to finds from the Geometric period and later finds, including sculpture from all periods of Naxos' history.

The Archaeological Museum of Naxos is one of the most important museums in the world due to its early Cycladic collections. It boasts of unique works of art and objects of daily use from Naxos and the so-called Little Cyclades complex of (Schoinoussa, Donoussa, Koufonissia, Keros-Daskalio, and Iraklia), which highlight the history of the Aegean region.

The collections on display includes jewelry, art, pottery, statues, vessels with inscriptions, sculptures, glassware, etc. from different parts of the Greek Island."[18-19]

Mr and Mrs McGregor were shown around the museum, and they saw the wide range of collections displayed that tell the story of the Island of Naxos, and other Greek Islands. They were also able to spot a bit of resemblance and similarities with some of the Naxos

Museum items compared with the ones they saw at the Museum of Prehistoric Thera, in Fira, Santorini, Greece last week.

They finished their tour of the Naxos Museum and Apollos took them to a shop where they got a few souvenirs. After that, he drove them to the port of Naxos, which is situated on the western side of the Island in the capital town of Chora, to board their ferry back to Santorini. They thanked Apollos for his services, and said goodbye to him.

They got on board their ferry and were glad they visited Naxos. They went to the dining area and served themselves delicious food, fresh fruit juice, and water. After their meal, they sat next to each other. Mary rested her head on Shaun's shoulder while he drew her closer properly and wrapped his hand around her.

In just about 1 hour 45 minutes, they are safely back to Athinios port in Santorini. Aristarchos was already there waiting to take them. They got into the car, and he drove them back to their Perfecto 5-star hotel. They thanked Aristarchos and said goodbye to him.

As they got into their suite, Shaun prayed briefly to thank God for a safe journey to and from Naxos.

Shaun asked his wife, "How did you find the trip to Naxos?

She replied, "Awesome! I love it. It's a good addition to my honeymoon memories. I'm glad we visited the museum."

They turned the television to the *Christian Broadcasting Network (CBN)* and started listening to

News while they sat on the soft upholstery sofa relaxing. After a while, they decided to do their Bible reaching for the day. So they got out their Bibles and notebooks and sat down. Shaun said, "I am doing a brief teaching on the subject:

FINISH THE TASK

The reason why I chose this topic is because many people start things, but they don't finish the task, or project, and that is not good, and it also reveals that the person does not have full determination, zeal, and commitment to complete the project.

Finishing a task, business, or project is as important as starting it. And finishing is even more important because it's only when you finish that you can start enjoying the full benefits. As long as the task is half done, and uncompleted, you are not likely to enjoy the full benefits of the task or project.

Jesus said in:

John 19:30

> *When Jesus therefore had received the vinegar, he said, <u>It is finished;</u> and he bowed his head, and gave up the ghost.* (Underline mine)

Jesus had one main task. And that was to die to save us. He accomplished that and said, *"It is finished"* just before He died. He completed the task.

The Apostle Paul is another person who fulfilled his purpose on earth before translating to be with the Lord. Read what he said in the scripture below.

2 *Timothy 4:7*

> *I have fought a good fight, <u>I have finished my course</u>, I have kept the faith:* (Underline mine)

King Solomon was also a finisher.

1 *Kings 6:38-1 Kings 7:1*

> *38. And in the eleventh year, in the month Bul, which is the eighth month, was the <u>house finished</u> throughout all the parts thereof, and according to all the fashion of it. So was he seven years in building it.*
>
> *7:1 But Solomon was building his own house thirteen years, and <u>he finished all his house</u>.* (Underline mine)

King Solomon started building the Temple of the Lord and his own house and finished it as you can see from the above scriptures. As Christians, we also have to start and finish our tasks. Avoid unfinished business, and uncompleted projects. When you start reading an article or a book, finish it. When you start a training or course, finish it. When you start a business, finish it. When you start a project, finish it. When you start eating, finish it. When you start a journey, finish it. When you start a marriage, finish it. No separation or divorce. When you start ...., finish it!

Some people are in the habit of not finishing whatever they start. They get so excited about owning a four bedroom house with a swimming pool, they buy it. And after a little while all the excitement is gone. They want another house. Some people are in the habit of starting a relationship and in no time all the excitement they had about this great lady or gentleman is gone. They marry and very soon they want separation and divorce. What had happened to this person they were madly in love with? Some are so excited about a job, business, car, church, school, country, etc. They get it, or get in and in no time all the excitement is gone. They lose interest, or are tired, or do not want to be committed anymore.

Something is wrong here with this kind of attitude and trend. And my prayer is that the Most High God will help us all in Jesus' name. Tell yourself powerfully, "I will always start and finish my tasks by the grace of God in Jesus' name. Amen!"

When Shaun finished his teaching, Mary stood up and started clapping and said, "Honey, this is a very powerful teaching. I have resolved that this marriage for me is till death do us part. I made the wedding vow, and I mean it."

Shaun replied, "Absolutely the same here. By the special grace of God, this marriage is till death do us part. No separation, no divorce."

Mary said, "Honey, can I ask a question?"

Shaun replied, "Of course you can, darling?"

QUESTION

Mary asked, "What should a person or a couple do to start and finish their tasks?

ANSWER

Shaun replied, "I have already given most of the answers in my teaching, but I would like to emphasize and add that you should be sincere to yourself not to start a task you know you can't finish. And when you start, be fully determined and committed to finish. Avoid laziness. Be diligent. Remain focused and avoid distractions. Your motto should be: *"I must finish this task."*

Mary said, "Thank you very much for that brilliant answer."

They got ready and went to the restaurant to have a light dinner. They got back to their suite and sat down in front of the television and tuned in to *TBN,* and they listened to the preaching of *Pastor Joel Osteen.*

After that, they prayed, changed into their nightwear, and got on the bed, kissed and slept.

CHAPTER TEN

DAY 10 – TUESDAY
ORGASM AND SEX IN MARRIAGE

They got up in the morning feeling great. They exchanged good morning greetings and washed their teeth and tongues, and came out to the sitting room with their Bibles and notebooks ready for their morning devotion. And as their custom is, they started thanking, praising, and worshiping God. They also made powerful scriptural declarations, and then prayed in tongues.

As they finished doing this, Shaun said, my teaching for today is titled:

MALE ORGASM AND SEX IN MARRIAGE

What is orgasm?

The Merriam-Webster dictionary gives the meaning of orgasm as, "Intense or paroxysmal excitement; especially: the rapid pleasurable release of neuromuscular tensions at the height of sexual arousal that is usually accompanied by the ejaculation of semen in the male and by vaginal contractions in the female."

Of what use is a marriage honeymoon if husband and wife do not have sexual intercourse, and experience orgasm? Is this not part of what will help create excitement, pleasure, and joy, plus enhance oneness, intimacy, and procreation in marriage? We will therefore explore here how orgasm can be achieved.

Male orgasm and sex

The main functions of the male orgasm are enjoyment and sperm ejaculation. Multiple hormones, nerve pathways, and organs are involved in the male orgasm. Male testicles produce testosterone, which promotes sexual libido and causes arousal. Men usually rely on physical stimulation for arousal.

Generally, orgasm in men refers to the peak of sexual fulfillment whereby blood flows to the genitals, and the muscles become tense during arousal, and this is followed by ejaculation during sex. The ejaculated semen comprises sperm cells and the seminal fluid which carries them.

TYPES OF MALE ORGASMS

Let us look at the following four types of male orgasms.

Ejaculatory orgasm: This is the standard orgasm that most men experience during intercourse. When a man is sexually aroused, blood flows to the penis, causing it to be erect. Muscle contractions help to push semen into the urethra for ejaculation.

Blended orgasm: This happens when multiple areas of the male body experience pleasure at the same time. The key is to stimulate as many of the erogenous zones as possible during foreplay or intercourse.

Multiple orgasms: To have sequential multiple orgasms, you must orgasm and take some rest during the refractory period in order to be strengthened.

Pelvic orgasm: Pelvic orgasm involves a method called edging. You will be in control of the orgasm, and prolong the sexual experience. There will also be a contraction of the pelvic floor muscles.

CAUSES OF MALE ORGASM

Intercourse: The male orgasm usually occurs when a man is having intercourse, and the contractions in the pelvic and genital muscles force the body to expel the semen. Continuous stimulation of different erogenous zones like the genitals, nipples, and kissing leads to orgasm.

Oral sex with your spouse is another way that leads to orgasm. This replicates the experience of sexual intercourse.

Masturbation is another way of achieving male orgasm, but you must not do that as a Christian because of the negative impact it will have on your spiritual life. Flee from masturbation.

PHASES OF THE MALE ORGASM

The male orgasm can be classified into five phases as follows:

Desire: This is a main aspect of a healthy sexuality. This phase entails that the man should eagerly anticipate, fantasize, and long for sex, as well believe that sex will satisfy him and his spouse in the marriage.

Arousal: When a man perceives sexual interest, the brain sends a signal to the sex organs through the spinal cord to cause an erection. The penis erects when blood fills the spongy tissue facilitated by arteries. The scrotum also pulls towards the body.

Plateau: In this stage, the pelvic thrusts become more intense and involuntary. As the thrusting picks up speed, the heart rate can go up to 175 beats per minute. Men might also experience a rise in body temperature and blood pressure. The duration of the plateau phase ranges from 30 seconds to 120 seconds.

Orgasm: During the orgasm stage, men experience ejaculation. The semen is ejaculated from the body due to contractions of the muscles. The reward center of the brain receives a bunch of neurochemicals during orgasm and triggers an intense emotional response. After the orgasm, the body prepares for the final phase.

Resolution and refraction: The penis loses the erection slowly after ejaculation. With the reduction in muscle tension, men feel more relaxed and even sleepy. Most men will have a resting or refractory period after the orgasm, and they will not be able to reach an orgasmic state during this time. The period varies from man to man, depending on their age. For younger men, it can last for half an hour to one hour, while older men can even need a day to recover completely.

BENEFITS OF THE MALE ORGASM

Enhances brain functioning: During an orgasm, the brain experiences an increased blood flow, which helps to enhance its abilities. The heightened oxygen utilization and nutrient intake during male orgasm provide the brain with a boost. You might find yourself more receptive to learning a tough topic after an orgasm.

Reduces the risk of prostate cancer: According to a 2004 study by the National Cancer Institute, the male test subjects who had more than 21 orgasms every month were 30% less likely to suffer from prostate cancer as compared to the ones who experienced fewer than seven orgasms. The reason behind this is not very clear, but one theory states that orgasming often rids the prostate of old semen, which could otherwise turn carcinogenic.

Reduces stress: The male body releases endorphins and oxytocin during an orgasm, which can boost someone's mood instantly. If you are going through a stressful period, an orgasm will take your mind off it for a while. You will end up feeling relaxed and comfortable.

Pain relief: The oxytocin released during the male orgasm can alleviate pain and ache, even if it is for a temporary period. If you are looking for some immediate relief, then opting for an orgasm could be the solution.

MALE ORGASM DISORDERS

Male orgasm disorder can cause a lot of stress and anxiety in men. Orgasm disorders are not synonymous with ejaculation disorders.

Dry orgasm: This is a male orgasm disorder that causes men to ejaculate very little semen during their orgasm. This can be frustrating as it leaves the sexual experience lacking. This condition can affect a man trying for a child with his spouse. This condition can be the result of sperm duct blockage.

Anorgasmia: This is a condition in which a man is unable to orgasm and can be worrisome. It might be triggered by certain psychological problems like trauma, and stress. To treat anorgasmia, first determine the root cause.

Causes of male orgasm disorder: Problems like diabetes, hypertension, and some medicines can lead to it.

BARRIERS TO MALE ORGASM

Not being able to orgasm can be distressing for anyone, regardless of gender. For men, it can be especially taxing. Orgasms and ejaculation usually occur simultaneously. They are, however, in fact two separate events. This means you can ejaculate without having the orgasmic experience, and have what is known as a dry orgasm.

Without an erection there cannot be orgasm and ejaculation. The following things can make a man's penis remain in a flaccid state without an erection: Lack of libido, fears, acute poverty, insult from spouse, cold weather, and a distracted mindset.

Note that because most people experience ejaculation and orgasm at the same time, it can be referred to as a combined experience. Our sexual function fluctuates, which means things like sexual desire, erectile function and orgasm abilities, change. There are chances that some of the things we go through, like 'delayed ejaculation,' can resolve themselves.

Reasons for male difficulty reaching orgasm

Sexual fantasies: Some people have more exciting masturbation, or pornographic fantasies about someone else apart from their spouse during sex. You must give up such habits because they inhibit orgasm. You must focus on your spouse, spirit, soul, and body. Don't practice and get addicted to masturbation and pornography as a Christian because it will greatly affect your spiritual growth and maturity.

Don't use masturbation and pornography to teach your body and brain a wrong specific way to have an orgasm, which simply cannot be replicated with your spouse during sexual intercourse.

When you stop masturbation and pornography, it will help restore your ability to experience orgasm with your spouse. If you are finding it hard to stop, then you may need to see a health professional like your doctor, a sexologist, or a sex therapist.

Communication: You have to communicate to your spouse your erogenous zones, and how you want her to touch them during foreplay and sex in order for you to have orgasm. If you don't communicate, that will contribute to difficulties in reaching orgasm.

My prayer is that the Lord will help everyone to achieve orgasm and ejaculation during sexual intercourse, which will lead to reproduction in Jesus' name."[20-22]

When he finished his teaching, Mary stood up smiling and clapping for Shaun and said, "Amen! Honey, this is a great teaching you've just given, and I am blessed to hear this teaching. Thank you very much."

Mary continued, "Honey, can I ask a question?"

Shaun replied, "Yes, of course you can."

QUESTION

Mary asked, "Honey, what are your erogenous zones so that I know where, and how to touch you during foreplay and sexual intercourse in order for you to experience orgasm and ejaculate?"

ANSWER

Shaun answered, "That's a very good question darling. My main erogenous zones are my genitals, ears, chest, and mouth during kissing. I really love oral sex, which is also known as fellatio or a blow job. A gentle passionate touch will lead me to orgasm and ejaculation. I also enjoy different sex positions."

Mary, "Thank you for that brilliant answer. Now I know where and how to touch you to cause orgasm and ejaculation."

Shaun said, "Honey, can you please also teach on the subject: Female orgasm and sex?"

Mary cleared her throat and began,

"FEMALE ORGASM AND SEX IN MARRIAGE

Orgasms are a great way to be intimate with both yourself and your spouse. These brief moments of pleasure offer a host of benefits, like helping you manage your menstrual symptoms, improving your fertility, and help you deal with various aches and pains. Orgasms come in a variety of shapes and sizes, and are a great way for you to get really familiar with your own body. Let's look at the following three types of orgasm:

Clitoral Orgasm

The clitoris is the female genital erectile erogenous organ at the anterior end of the vulva that lies at the junction of the labia minora, and above the urethra extending to the vagina. This organ contains numerous sensitive nerves that plays a major role in sexual arousal and pleasure in women.

The clitoris can be stimulated by navigating it during foreplay and sexual intercourse with the fingers or erected penis penetration right through to the vagina with moves. The clitoral hood is directly above the clitoris, which is a bundle of nerves that will play a huge role in a female orgasm. Achieving orgasm does not just happen. It involves experimenting with different types of moves to discover the part to stimulate and to bring you pleasure.

You really need to communicate to your spouse where and how to touch your clitoris in order for you to achieve orgasm and experience sexual pleasures. This can involve fingering, licking, and sucking of the clitoris. Try to keep your mind focused on what you're trying to achieve, instead of thinking about the anatomy of it all. You may not achieve orgasm if you focus on another person apart from your spouse, or get your mind wandering on irrelevant things that will distract you from having orgasm. Be involved and connected with your spouse during sexual intercourse with spirit, soul, and body. When you are in a missionary position, wrap your legs around your spouse, hold, and kiss him during intercourse and be connected with him emotionally and spiritually.

G-Spot Orgasm

The G-spot is a slang term for a special spot in your vagina with the potential to bring you some intense orgasms. You can find it (2.5 to 5.1 cm) in, along the upper/top wall of your vagina. This spot is typically spongy, puckered, and ridged, which makes it a bit easier to identify. When you're aroused, your G-spot will swell a bit and be easier to find.

You can achieve an orgasm on your own if you know where your G-spot is. Rub your fingers over the spot, playing around at different speeds and applying different amounts of pressure as you go. There's no exact formula to follow that will guarantee an orgasm. All you've got to do is to keep playing with yourself until you feel an intense wave of pleasure.

It's important for you to note here that you must not engage in masturbation and pornography as a Christian because it will greatly affect your spiritual growth and maturity. Avoid anal orgasm, and the use of sex toys as a Christian. You may need to see your doctor or a sex therapist for help.

Help your spouse find your G-spot with their fingers or communicate it to him. For hygiene purposes, he must wash his hands before fingering you. Sit down or lie flat and separate your legs, which will make it easier for your spouse to explore. Guide their fingers to where your G-spot is, so they know what they're working with.

Try different moves and positions in bed to reach orgasm. Experiment with your spouse and find something that works well for you and your personal needs. Invite your spouse to massage your G-spot or play around with different amounts of pressure as they pleasure the area. Try different sex positions, like the missionary style, doggy style, and cowgirl style.

Cervical Orgasm

The cervix is located at the very top of the vaginal canal and can be stimulated by your spouse with deep penis penetration to produce orgasm. This may involve trying different positions to find one that allows for deep penetration. You must also speak to your spouse if you are in an uncomfortable position that hurts you.

WHAT HAPPENS DURING A FEMALE ORGASM?

During a true, full female orgasm, there is a combination of muscle contractions, biomechanical functions, and neurological chemistry. Your pelvic floor, uterus, and vagina all contract, and your brain is flooded with feel-good chemicals like oxytocin, serotonin, opiate, and dopamine.

BARRIERS TO FEMALE ORGASM

Reaching orgasm can be a complex and sometimes frustrating experience for many women. This challenge can stem from a variety of factors, including physical, emotional, and psychological influences. However, understanding your body, improving communication with your spouse, and exploring new techniques can significantly enhance your ability to achieve orgasm.

Other reasons women may have difficulty with orgasm include age, hormonal status, bad sexual experience, vaginismus experiences, no physical stimulation, general health, type of stimulation, the kind of sexual activity engaged like masturbation and pornography, and whether the relationship is a brief encounter or long-term.

The most common overall reasons given by women for difficulty with orgasm in a study carried out were stress and anxiety. The study covered the following areas:

- I am not interested in sex with my spouse.
- My spouse does not seem to be interested in sex with me.
- I do not enjoy sex with my spouse.
- My partner does not seem to enjoy sex with me.
- I am not sufficiently aroused/stimulated during sex.
- I am not adequately lubricated during sex.
- I experience pain and/or irritation during sex.
- We do not have enough time for sex.
- I am uncomfortable or self-conscious about my body/appearance.
- I feel that medication or a medical condition interferes with having an orgasm.
- I feel that my stress and/or anxiety make it difficult to have an orgasm.

Looking at the above list, the most common overall reasons given by women were stress and anxiety; followed by lack of arousal or stimulation; not enough time; pain or irritation during sex; insufficient lubrication; and medication-related problems.

It's better to start working on yourself, and also with the support of your spouse, to improve on your ability to orgasm rather than just making excuses, and doing nothing. Always ensure you are not shy about speaking to your spouse regarding sexual matters affecting you so that he can support you.

Some solutions to barriers to female orgasm

- Effective communication with your spouse.
- Try different sex-style positions.
- Forgive any traumatic sexual experience like rape.
- A change of any medication that inhibits orgasm.
- Stop masturbation and pornography.
- Focus on your spouse wholeheartedly, emotionally, and spiritually.

My prayer is that the Lord will help every woman, and couple to achieve orgasm during sexual intercourse which will lead to reproduction in Jesus' name."[23-25]

When she finished her teaching, Shaun stood up smiling and clapping for Mary and said, "Amen! Honey, this is a fantastic teaching you've just given, and I am blessed to hear this teaching. More wisdom, anointing, and grace upon your life. Thank you very much darling."

Shaun said, "Honey, can I ask some questions?"

Mary replied, "Yes, you can, darling."

QUESTION

Shaun asked, "Honey, what are your erogenous zones so that I know where, and how to touch you during foreplay and sexual intercourse in order for you to experience orgasm and sexual pleasures?"

ANSWER

Mary answered, "That's a very good question darling. My main erogenous zones are my genital, breasts, nipples, and mouth during kissing. I really love oral sex as in cunnilingus. A gentle passionate fingering and sucking of my clitoris that will lead me to orgasm. I also enjoy different sex positions."

Shaun said, "Thank you for that brilliant answer. Now I know where and how to touch you to cause orgasm."

QUESTION

Shaun continued and asked, "Is the Bible against oral sex in marriage?"

ANSWER

Mary answered, "That's another good question, and the answer is: No, the Bible is not against oral sex for legally married couples. However, oral sex must be consensual with the couple agreeing to do it. Don't force it on your spouse. And for hygiene purposes, take a good bath and thoroughly clean the genitals before you do it. Note also that oral sex should not replace sexual intercourse for reproduction purposes. I am glad that you asked this question so that some people will not think we are being immoral for having oral sex or sexual intercourse as a married couple."

Shaun replied, "Absolutely fantastic answer. Thank you very much darling."

This brings to an end their morning devotion. Mr and Mrs McGregor started undressing to take a shower. They are also ready for action to practice what they preached.

As they got into the bathroom, they started praising each other's great attractive bodies. They washed one another's body, chatting, touching, and laughing. They finished their bath and went straight to the bedroom, caressing, and kissing.

Shaun started touching Mary's erogenous zones, concentrating on licking and sucking her breasts and nipples, kissing, and gently licking and sucking her clitoris. And as he did this, he got words of approval from his wife, "Please give me more of it. I love you. Oh my God, you are the best husband in the world. Please suck my clitoris well. Yes, that's the point. Yeah, you got it. Thank you honey."

Mary also started touching Shaun's erogenous zones and then grabbed his penis and started licking and sucking it, and he said, "That's it. You are getting it. Please give me more darling. I love you."

Having done all these foreplays, they are now properly aroused, and she is well lubricated, and Shaun penetrated her and they started making love. They engaged in different sex-style positions until they had orgasm, got tired, and slept off.

They got up, cleaned up and dressed up and went down to the restaurant and had a delicious meal.

Shaun turned the TV on and *Bishop John Barnes* was preaching on the subject: *The love story of Ruth and Boaz*. This captured their attention and they listened attentively to the preaching.

After the sermon, Shaun said, "I like Ruth. She was a very faithful, and diligent woman, and I am glad the Lord blessed her in the end with a wealthy husband, Boaz."

Mary replied, "Yes, Ruth was indeed a faithful woman, and thank God for Naomi, a good mother-in-law who was there to mentor her. She married Boaz, a wealthy man."

She came close to Shaun and held him and said, "I am also glad God gave me a wealthy husband. Thank you, Honey, for marrying me."

Shaun looked at her beautiful face and replied, "You are welcome, my beautiful queen. You are a woman of substance and excellence. I am truly blessed to have you as my queen."

They held each other and started kissing and cuddling.

Shaun asked her, "Would you have married me if I was a poor man?"

They both started laughing. And she replied, "I don't answer hypothetical questions."

Mary continued, "I was greatly motivated when I found out that you are a wealthy man. Prior to that, your Scottish accent was a put off for me, but it has all gone unnoticed to me now."

They both started laughing again.

And Shaun said, "This Scottish accent! I thank God you still accepted me, my queen."

Mary replied, "It would have been a tough decision for me to make. My parents liked you so much when they saw you in Edinburgh, especially my Dad. My Dad asked me if I like you, and I said, 'Yes.' He said, 'Then forget about his accent and marry him.' He and my mum both said they like you. You were already winning. My Dad was ready to bless me and give me away to you. And I said, I will respect that because I know my daddy loves me a lot, and he would never want to give me away to any man that will hurt me. Look now, I am happily married to you. This is the best decision I have ever made. Thank you, my king."

Shaun replied, "You are welcome my beautiful lovely queen. Now that you've told me this story, we will visit your parents in Manchester and really bless them for approving our marriage."

Mary said, "That will be great. Thank you, my king."

They got dressed and went down to the restaurant to have their dinner. They had their luscious meal and went back to their suite. They put on the TV and tuned to *God channel* while they sat on the sitting room sofa next to each other.

After a while, they prayed, changed into their nightwear, and went to bed, kissed, and slept.

CHAPTER ELEVEN

DAY 11 – WEDNESDAY
ENDURE AFFLICTIONS IN
MARRIAGE AND LIFE

Mr and Mrs McGregor woke up and exchanged good morning greetings to each other, and embraced one another.

Shaun asked his wife, "How was your night?" She replied, "Great!"

They both quickly brushed their teeth and tongues, and got ready for their morning devotion. They brought out their Bibles and notebooks. And as their usual custom, they started thanking, praising, and worshipping God and then made scriptural declarations, and prayed in tongues.

Mary said, "Today is our fasting day, and I will be teaching on the topic:

ENDURE AFFLICTIONS IN MARRIAGE AND LIFE

What is affliction?

This is simply a state of being in great pain, suffering, or distress.

It is important to note that biblically we also have self-affliction. This is fasting, which is also referred to as affliction of the soul in:

Leviticus 16:31

> *It shall be a sabbath of rest unto you, <u>and ye shall afflict your souls</u>, by a statute for ever.* (Underline mine)

See below how the AMPC put the above scripture.

Leviticus 16:31 – (Amplified Bible – Classic Edition (AMPC)

> *It is a sabbath of [solemn] rest to you, <u>and you shall afflict yourselves [by fasting</u> with penitence and humiliation]; it is a statute forever.* (Underline mine)

See Leviticus 16:29 & 31, Leviticus 23:27 & 32, Numbers 29:7, and Isaiah 58:3 showing affliction of the soul, and it is also fasting. Today is our fasting day, so we will afflict / discipline our souls.

> *One of the reasons why I am doing this teaching today on this topic is because we live in a world full of impatient people who do not want to endure afflictions especially in marriage. Any little thing, they will separate and file for a divorce. Marriage means nothing to these kinds of people, and they lack respect for their spouse, and also lack the fear of God. The sad part of these kinds of erratic actions is that people who dabble into marriage without adequate knowledge and understanding of what marriage is about are the ones who usually act in this manner. And after acting in a terrible way, they will blame the devil. My friend, take responsibility*

for your actions and stop blaming the devil. Besides, when they divorce and marry another person, they start regretting their action because the person they divorced is better than the new person they married. The main problem is that they just can't even endure little afflictions in marriage and life. Remember 1 Peter 5:10 says, paraphrasing – "...After you've suffered/endured affliction for a while, God will perfect, establish, strengthen, and settle you." Pressure before pleasure. No test, no testimony.
2 Timothy 4:5

But watch thou in all things, <u>endure afflictions</u>, do the work of an evangelist, make full proof of thy ministry. (Underline mine)

The above scripture encourages us to endure afflictions.

2 Timothy 2:3

Thou therefore <u>endure hardness</u>, as a good soldier of Jesus Christ. (Underline mine)

The above verse also encourages us to endure hardness as good soldiers of Jesus Christ. Don't be lazy! Don't be afraid! Don't be a coward! You are a soldier of Jesus Christ. Be strong and of good courage in marriage and life.

Psalm 34:19

Many are the afflictions of the righteous: but the LORD delivereth him out of them all.

The above scripture gives us the guarantee that the Lord will deliver us out of all the afflictions we go through in marriage and life. Thank God for this verse.

John 16:33

> *These things I have spoken unto you, that in me ye might have peace. In the world ye shall have tribulation: but be of good cheer; I have overcome the world.*

My friend, cheer up! Laugh and dance. Jesus says He has taken care of the tribulations and afflictions in the above verse.

Some examples of people who went through afflictions in marriage and life

Abraham and Sarah had Isaac at the ages of 100 & 90 respectively. How many married couples will endure till that age before having a child today without separation and divorce? As if that is not enough, God ordered Abraham to offer Isaac his son, who he loved, as a sacrifice. Tough, but he did it. Is this not endurance?

Isaac and Rebekah had Esau and Jacob after 20 years of barrenness. Isaac married Rebekah when he was 40 years old and had twins at age 60. See Genesis 25:19-26. How many married couples will endure 20 years without a child today, and without separation, divorce, or a second wife? Is this not the endurance of barrenness affliction in marriage?

Job lost everything he had in chapter 1 of his book. Yes, he lost everything! Things got so bad that he was smote with sore boils all over his body, and his wife told him to curse God and die. See Job 2:9. Is this not a terrible affliction in life? Job endured all the afflictions, and in the end, God gave him a double blessing. See Job 42:10.

Hannah was barren, and her mate Peninnah provoked and mocked her. But she endured all the afflictions and remained steadfast in her prayers, and God answered, and she conceived and gave birth to Prophet Samuel. Is this not a terrible affliction in marriage?

Naomi and family relocated to Moab because of famine. She lost her husband and two sons in a foreign land, Moab. See Ruth 1. Is this not a terrible affliction in marriage and life? But she endured the afflictions.

Paul and Silas were locked up in a prison and their feet secured in the stocks for preaching the gospel. They did not complain. They endured the afflictions. And at midnight they prayed and sang praises. And an earthquake struck that shook the foundations of the prison, and the doors opened, and their bands loosed. See Acts 16:24 -26.

The Apostle Paul gave a catalog of the things he suffered in ministry in 2 Corinthians 11:23-27. He also suffered a thorn in the flesh by the messenger of Satan to buffet him in 2 Corinthians 12:7. He endured the afflictions.

THINGS TO NOTE ABOUT AFFLICTIONS

Afflictions are not totally bad. It involves a process of crushing, trials, tribulations, purging, and refining in a furnace similar to removing impurities from silver and gold. Afflictions can be tests. And no test, no testimony.

As born-again Christians, we are made with supernatural materials. We are fearfully and wonderfully made. We are more than conquerors, and overcomers. Hence, we are to withstand the fiery darts of the enemy with our shield of faith, and endure afflictions as good soldiers of Christ. Perhaps you are facing a lot of challenges today, to the extent that you may be asking, "How, and when will all these afflictions be over?" This message is for you to endure afflictions. God is working behind the scenes to grant you all-round victory in Jesus' name.

Afflictions don't last forever. You pass through them.

Isaiah 43:2 says, "When thou passest through the water, I will be with thee; and through the rivers, they shall not overflow thee: when thou walkest through the fire, thou shalt not be burned; neither shall the flame kindle upon thee."

Anything that has a beginning must have an end including afflictions. No condition is permanent. So, my friends, pass through those afflictions knowing fully well that God is with you, and the afflictions will definitely be over one day.

God will not permit any affliction that will overwhelm you.

1 Corinthians 10:13 "There hath no temptation taken you but such as is common to man: but God is faithful, who will not suffer you to be tempted above that ye are able; but will with the temptation also make a way to escape, that ye may be able to bear it."

Afflictions are customized. The ones you go through are specifically designed only for you. The same goes for me. The good news is that the afflictions you go through are such that they are common to men. Not totally strange. And God allows it because He knows you can bear it successfully. Also, there is always a way of escape for the temptations we go through.

Affliction time is training time.

Psalm 119:71-72

> *71. It is good for me that I have been afflicted; that I might learn thy statutes.*

> *72 .The law of thy mouth is better unto me than thousands of gold and silver.*

The Psalmist is saying in the above verses that it was good that he was afflicted because it gave him the opportunity to read his Bible. Therefore, the affliction period is a time to study the Word of God and grow in wisdom – Training!

Afflictions bring forth promotion and glory of God.

After Shadrach, Meshach, and Abednego (SMA) successfully passed through the fire of the fiery furnace (affliction), the Bible recorded in:

Daniel 3:30 "Then the king promoted Shadrach, Meshach, and Abednego, in the province of Babylon." Your promotion is guaranteed after affliction in Jesus' name.

Isaiah 48:10

> *Behold, I have refined thee, but not with silver; I have chosen thee in the furnace of affliction.*

The furnace of affliction is a place of refinement. If you desire to be great in life, you must be determined to endure the afflictions you face in this furnace. You will be in prison and you will be fed with the bread of affliction and water of affliction. Anguish!

1 Kings 22:27

> *And say, Thus saith the king, Put this fellow in the <u>prison</u>, and feed him with <u>bread of affliction</u> and with <u>water of affliction</u>, until I come in peace.* (Underline mine)

Job 23:10

> *But he knoweth the way that I take: when he hath tried me, I shall come forth as gold.*

As stated in the above verse, the trials we go through in life will remove all impurities and cause us to be refined and shine like gold. The afflictions and refinement will make you a better person.

2 Corinthians 4:17

> *For our light affliction, which is but for a moment, worketh for us a far more exceeding and eternal weight of glory;*

Glory be to God. The Apostle Paul says in the above verse that the afflictions we go through are light and also for a moment. The afflictions will also bring great glory to us and God in Jesus' name.

Solutions to afflictions - Pray

James 5:13 - Is any among you afflicted? let him pray. Is any merry? let him sing psalms.

As you pray, be encouraged and note that God does have mercy on the afflicted – Isaiah 49:13; God delivers the poor in affliction - Job 36:15; God sees the affliction of His people – Exodus 3:7; God stops afflictions – Zephaniah 3:19.

Note that you must not complain during afflictions.

Job went through a series of afflictions. He lost everything he had. Yes, everything! But he did not complain or blame God by asking "why me?" *Job 1:22 says "In all this Job sinned not, nor charged God foolishly."*

Jesus Christ of Nazareth was afflicted seriously for our sake. And the Bible states in:

Isaiah 53:7 "He was oppressed, and he was afflicted, yet he opened not his mouth: he is brought as a lamb to the slaughter, and as a sheep before her shearers is dumb, so he openeth not his mouth." - To complain.

This is what to "endure affliction" means, and that's what gives victory. Instead of complaining, open your mouth and give God all the praise and glory. Praise God the way Paul and Silas did it in Acts 16.

My prayer for you today is that the Lord will see you through any affliction or challenge you may be facing in Jesus' name. God will endow you with the grace and wisdom to overcome every challenge. With your eyes you will see every enemy, and challenge crumble and be destroyed in the mighty name of Jesus. I declare permanent victory for you in Jesus' name. Amen!

After the teaching, Shaun stood up and started clapping for his wife and said, "Amen! This teaching is the absolute truth, and I am blessed to listen to it. Thank you very much and more grace, anointing, and wisdom upon your life darling."

Mary replied, "Amen!"

The morning devotion ended, and they started undressing and went straight to the bathroom and had their bath.

Today is a fasting day for them. They decided to do their own personal Bible studies, meditation, and have a special quiet time with God. They did this for 5 hours without talking to each other. At 4 pm they decided to stop.

And then Mary said, "Honey, did God say anything to you?"

Shaun replied, "Yes. He gave us

Hebrews 13:5

> *Let your conversation be without covetousness; and be content with such things as ye have: for he hath said, I will never leave thee, nor forsake thee."*

Mary said aloud, "Oh my God, He gave me the same scripture." She brought out her notebook and showed it to the husband where she wrote it down. Shaun also showed her his notebook where he wrote his own down. What a confirmation. What He says to one, He says to another. They both rejoiced for the word.

They decide to dress up and take a walk around the town of Fira, for sightseeing.[26] They set off holding hands and chatting about their getting together as a couple and what their expectations are for the future. They saw the beautiful streets, buildings, people, and admired the serenity in the environment. As they got back, they went to the restaurant and broke their fast for the day and finally went back to their suite.

They put on their TV and tuned in to *TBN* channel, and *Pastor Creflo Dollar* is also preaching on the subject: Afflictions. Whao! They listened with rapt attention, and Shaun commented, "Honey, he is also making reference to the scriptures you used in our morning devotion. This is one Spirit indeed."

Mary replied, "It is one Holy Spirit indeed. God is using him to emphasize the message. We must endure afflictions as a couple."

They had their shower again, changed into their nightwear, and went to bed, kissed, and slept.

CHAPTER TWELVE

DAY 12 – THURSDAY
DEALING WITH THE WORKS OF
THE FLESH

They got up in the morning feeling strong and refreshed. They quickly got ready and started their morning devotion by thanking, praising, and worshiping the Lord. They also made powerful scriptural declarations, and then prayed in tongues.

Shaun said, "Today, I will be teaching on the subject:

DEALING WITH THE WORKS OF THE FLESH

It's interesting to note how Christians including couples accuse, and blame the devil for things he is not responsible for. We need to really discipline ourselves by walking in the Spirit, rather than the flesh. The Bible says in:

Galatians 5:19-21

> [19] **Now the works of the flesh are manifest,** *which are these; Adultery, fornication, uncleanness, lasciviousness,*

> [20] *Idolatry, witchcraft, hatred, variance, emulations, wrath, strife, seditions, heresies,*

²¹ *Envyings, murders, drunkenness, revellings, and such like: of the which I tell you before, as I have also told you in time past, that **they which do such things shall not inherit the kingdom of God.*** (Emphasis mine)

Verse 19 above says "***Now the works of the flesh are......***" It didn't say, "***Now the works of the devil are.....***" Look at the long list. What a lot of Christians call the work of the devil is not. Perhaps people don't read their Bible well to find out the truth, or they simply want to ignore the truth and blame the devil for every mishap. But this should not be so. We need to accept responsibility for our own mistakes. This is the only way we can grow, and become mature Christians.

Note that Apostle Paul wrote this epistle to the Galatian church Christians. They are born-again Christians, but they still indulge in the above-listed works of the flesh, and this means they are carnal or sensual Christians. We must grow and mature to be spiritual Christians.

After looking at the above long list, it's important to do an honest self-examination, and identify those works of the flesh that need to be dealt with in your life now, then go ahead and start doing the right things to fix them through the power of the Holy Spirit. No procrastination. Remember the last part of verse 21 above says that, "*.....they which do such things shall not inherit the kingdom of God.*" That's talking about heaven.

HOW DO YOU DEAL WITH THE WORKS OF THE FLESH?

Walk in the Spirit

One main thing to do in order to deal with the works of the flesh is to walk in the Spirit. *Galatians 5:16 says, "This I say then, Walk in the Spirit, and ye shall not fulfil the lust of the flesh."* Some of the things we have to do in order to walk in the Spirit includes to do Bible study, meditate, and practice what the Bible says because it's the sword of the Spirit according to Ephesians 6:17. We also have to pray, praise, and fellowship with other believers. It's also important to keep on abstaining from sin.

Discipline yourself

It's also vital to keep on disciplining yourself. *1 Corinthians 9:27 says, "But I keep under my body, and bring it into subjection: lest that by any means, when I have preached to others, I myself should be a castaway."* Apostle Paul says in this scripture that he disciplines his body. We also have to do the same as Christians by saying no to the works of the flesh no matter how enticing they may appear to be. Be in full control of your flesh, and not your flesh in control of you as a Christian. It can be done because we are more than conquerors, and overcomers in Jesus' name.

Die daily

The Apostle Paul said in *1 Corinthians 15:31,* "... *I die daily.*" You must be prepared to die daily to bad habits and character, sin, and all evil. Give up the worldly lifestyle, and remain focused as a born-again Christian.

Renewed mindset and consciousness

The Bible says in: *Proverbs 23:7*, *"For as he thinketh in his heart, so is he:…"*

Philippians 2:5, "Let this mind be in you, which was also in Christ Jesus:"

Romans 12:2, "And be not conformed to this world: but be ye transformed by the renewing of your mind, that ye may prove what is that good, and acceptable, and perfect, will of God."

Romans 8:9, "But ye are not in the flesh, but in the Spirit, if so be that the Spirit of God dwell in you. Now if any man have not the Spirit of Christ, he is none of his."

1 Corinthians 6:17, "But he that is joined unto the Lord is one spirit."

Galatians 5:25, "If we live in the Spirit, let us also walk in the Spirit."

As stated in the above scriptures, we must always think, believe, and have the consciousness that we are born-again Christians, filled with the Holy Spirit, and therefore not in the flesh, but in the Spirit in Jesus' name. Amen!"

When he finished his teaching, she stood up and started smiling and clapping for Shaun and said, "Amen! I am truly blessed by this teaching. Hopefully people will quit blaming the devil for the bad things that happen, and focus on putting their flesh into subjection."

They ended the morning devotion and started getting ready to go to the gym for exercise. They got to the gym and went straight to the treadmill machines next to each other and first started walking and then increased it to light jogging. When they were done on the treadmills, they got on the bicycle exercise machines. They are more interested in cardiovascular exercises that will help with the efficient heart functions and circulation of blood.

They went into the swimming pool. The water is very clean and at the right temperature. The morning sun is also rising making the pool look nice. They started from the shallow end and moved on to the deep parts. They both know how to swim so they worked well and enjoyed it together. When they got tired and satisfied, they left back to their suite.

They got into the bathroom and had a quick shower and dressed up and went down to the restaurant to eat. After their delicious meal, they went back to their suite.

They sat down on the sitting room sofa and turned on their TV to the *TBN* channel.

Shaun asked her, "How are you finding the honeymoon so far?"

She replied, "Splendid! I am enjoying every bit of it."

Shaun said, "That's good. Are you happy with the way your husband is treating you so far?"

Mary answered, "Yes oh! You are really treating me well. You are the best husband in the world. Thank you very much for all your love and care."

Shaun replied, "You are welcome sweetheart. If you need anything, just let me know."

Mary said, "Really?"

Shaun replied, "Sure."

Mary said, "Please give me one billion pounds."

Shaun said aloud, "Hey, this woman, do you want to kill me? One billion pounds?"

They both started laughing, cuddling, and kissing.

Mary said, "But you said if I need anything I should let you know."

Shaun replied, "I know. But that's too much."

Mary replied, "Oh, you thought I would ask for peanuts from my lord and king? No way!"

They both started laughing out aloud again, cuddling, caressing, and kissing. And as they continued with this foreplay, Shaun got a full erection, and they both started undressing and got into the bedroom. Shaun started sucking her breasts, and kissing her as she lay in the missionary position, and then he penetrated her and started making love to her and then ejaculated. He got up and cleaned up.

Shaun started massaging her. He started touching her on every part of her body from her feet to her head, especially her erogenous zones, and also kissing her on every part of her body.

Mary said, "Thank you very much honey. I am really enjoying this massaging and kissing you are giving me."

Shaun replied, "This professional massaging service is not free."

Mary asked, "How much?"

Shaun replied, "One billion pounds."

Mary said aloud, "You this man, are you serious?"

Shaun replied, "Yes!"

Mary said, "I will pay five billion pounds."

They both started laughing out aloud.

And Shaun got a full erection again. She positioned herself in the doggy-style position, and he started making love to her so intensely until he ejaculated. They changed their sex position to the cowgirl style while they looked at each other, smiling, and kissing, while she maneuvered the sex session the way she wanted and after a while, they got tired, disengaged, and slept off. Lovely romance, love, and sex session.

They got up in the evening, had a shower, dressed up, and went to the restaurant to have their delicious dinner. They got back to their suite and sat on the sofa in their sitting room, and turned on the TV and tuned to the *TBN* channel and *Bishop T D Jakes* came on preaching.

After the preaching on TV, they prayed, changed into their nightwear, got on the bed, kissed and slept off.

CHAPTER THIRTEEN

DAY 13 – FRIDAY
THANKSGIVING, PRAISE, AND WORSHIP

Mr and Mrs McGregor got up in the morning feeling very strong and healthy as always. They quickly prepared and got together for their morning devotion.

Shaun said to his wife, "Honey, today's morning devotion is going to be a bit different because we are only going to do one thing together today, and that's

THANKSGIVING, PRAISE, AND WORSHIP.

Mary replied, "That's perfectly fine with me darling."

Shaun continued, "The word 'Thanksgiving' is a compound word made up of two words, 'Thanks' and 'Giving.' Therefore, I will sow a seed now to thank the Most High God because it is better to thank and honor the Lord with our mouth, and also back it up with our substance offering."

He immediately transferred a special seed of thanksgiving of £70,000 into Shekinah Pentecostal Church account, and said, "Thank you, Jesus, for everything you do for me and my wife. We are grateful."

When Mary saw her husband do that, she also followed her husband's good example and transferred a special seed of thanksgiving of £1,000 into Shekinah Pentecostal Church account, and also said, "Thank you, Jesus, for everything you do for me and my husband. We are grateful."

Shaun continued saying,

"What is thanksgiving, praise, and worship?

This is simply a sincere acknowledgment, appreciation, honor, and adoration of the awesomeness, glory, and power of the Most High God with our mouth, clapping, dancing, substance, instruments, and the right attitude, because they that worship Him must do so in spirit and in truth. The Bible says in:

Isaiah 43:21

> *This people have I formed for myself; they shall shew forth my praise.*

God created us to praise and worship Him as stated in the scripture above. Right from the beginning when God created Adam and Eve, and put them in the Garden of Eden, they had fellowship with God.

HOW DO WE THANK, PRAISE, AND WORSHIP GOD?

We are to open our mouth and speak

Psalm 34:1

> *I will bless the LORD at all times: his praise shall continually be in my mouth.*

The above scripture tells us that the praise of God should be in our mouth continually. We must continually acknowledge His Majesty, and thank Him for His mercies, grace, forgiveness, provisions, and protection. This means there is no room for complaints at all.

Ephesians 5:19

> *Speaking to yourselves in psalms and hymns and spiritual songs, singing and making melody in your heart to the Lord;*

The above scripture encourages us to speak the Psalms and hymns, and make melodies in our hearts unto the Lord.

Psalm 119:164

> *Seven times a day do I praise thee because of thy righteous judgments.*

Dance, sing, and clap your hands

2 Samuel 6:14

> *And David danced before the LORD with all his might; and David was girded with a linen ephod.*

Psalm 47:1

> *O clap your hands, all ye people; shout unto God with the voice of triumph.*

The above scriptures also declare we have to praise God by dancing, clapping our hands, singing, and shouting with a voice of triumph. Praise Him!

Musical instruments

Psalm 150

> [1] *Praise ye the LORD. Praise God in his sanctuary: praise him in the firmament of his power.*
>
> [2] *Praise him for his mighty acts: praise him according to his excellent greatness.*
>
> [3] *Praise him with the sound of the trumpet: praise him with the psaltery and harp.*
>
> [4] *Praise him with the timbrel and dance: praise him with stringed instruments and organs.*
>
> [5] *Praise him upon the loud cymbals: praise him upon the high sounding cymbals.*
>
> [6] *Let every thing that hath breath praise the LORD. Praise ye the LORD.*

Psalm 150 says we have to praise the Lord with all kinds of instruments. Shaun brought out his Saxophone and started playing:

Psalm 8:9

> *O LORD our Lord, how excellent is thy name in all the earth!*

Psalm 57:5

> *Be thou exalted, O God, above the heavens; let thy glory be above all the earth.*

Exodus 15:11

> *Who is like unto thee, O LORD, among the gods? Who is like thee, glorious in holiness, fearful in praises, doing wonders?*

Mary sang the songs, clapped, and danced as Shaun played the Saxophone. Awesome!

After a while, Shaun said, "This is great and wonderful indeed. Lord, we give you all the praise," and then he stopped. He continued, "The Bible says:

Thank, praise, and worship God in everything

1 Thessalonians 5:18

> *In every thing give thanks: for this is the will of God in Christ Jesus concerning you.*

When we thank, praise, and worship God in everything, all things will also begin to work together for our good – Romans 8:28, and our challenges turn to us for a testimony – Luke 21:13. Praise God!

Let's begin to thank God as follows:

Thank you, Lord, for keeping us alive and well.

Thank you, Lord, for all your protection and provision for us and our families.

Thank you, Lord, for our job, business, and ministry.

Thank you, Lord, for our Marketing manager job at the National bank.

Thank you, Lord, for our evangelical ministry.

Thank you, Lord, for our Oil and Gas Company.

Thank you, Lord, for the new massive contracts you are giving us.

Thank you, Lord, for the excellent employees you are giving to us.

Thank you, Lord, for your mercies and forgiveness.

Thank you, Lord, for the success of our marriage.

Thank you, Lord, for this honeymoon holiday.

Thank you, Lord, for a blissful marriage.

Thank you, Lord, because this marriage is till death do us part.

Thank you, Lord, for the fruit of the womb, males and females.

Thank you, Lord, for our homes.

Thank you, Lord, because no weapon formed against us and our family shall prosper – Isaiah 54:17.

Thank you, Lord, for fighting all our battles, seen and unseen Exodus - 14:14.

Thank you, Lord, because no evil shall befall us, neither shall any plague come near our dwelling – Psalm 91:10.

Thank you, Lord, for giving your angels charge over us – Psalm 91:11.

Thank you, Lord, for destroying the works of the devil – 1 John 3:8.

Thank you, Lord, for the restoration of everything the devil ever stole from us – Joel 2:25.

Thank you, Lord, for making us overcomers, more than conquerors, and victorious in Christ Jesus – 1 John 5:4; Romans 8:37.

Thank you, Lord, for causing the enemies that rose up against us to be defeated before us. They will come one way and flee in seven ways – Deut. 28:7.

Thank you, Lord, for granting us the power to tread upon serpents and scorpions and all the power of the enemy – Luke 10:19.

Thank you, Lord, because every arrow and missile of the enemy goes back to sender

Thank you, Lord, because he that digs a pit shall fall into their own pit – Psalm 7:15 & 9:15.

Thank you, Lord, because the swords of the enemies shall pierce through their own hearts and their bows shall be broken – Psalm 37:15.

Thank you, Lord, for preserving us from all evil, preserving our soul, and preserving our going out and coming in – Psalm 121:7-8.

Thank you, Lord, because we shall always go out with joy, and be led forth with peace – Isaiah 55:12.

Thank you, Lord, because all the challenges we go through in life shall turn to us for a testimony – Luke 21:13.

Thank you, Lord, for increasing us in wisdom and stature, and in favor with God and man – Luke 2:52.

Thank you, Lord, for filling us with more anointing and wisdom.

Thank you, Lord, for filling us continually with the Holy Ghost and power to do exploits for the kingdom of God – Acts 10:38.

Thank you, Lord, for filling us with the love of God which is shed abroad our hearts – Romans 5:5.

Thank you, Lord, for daily loading us with your benefits – Psalm 68:19.

Thank you, Lord, for blessing us with all spiritual blessings in heavenly places, and the blessings are manifesting – Ephesians 1:3.

Thank you, Lord, for opening the windows of heaven and releasing so much blessings to us so much that we don't have enough room to receive them – Malachi 3:10.

Thank you, Lord, for supplying all our need according to your riches in glory by Christ Jesus – Phil. 4:19.

Thank you, Lord, for coming to give us life, and giving it to us more abundantly – John 10:10.

Thank you, Lord, for filling us continually with the joy of the Lord which is our strength – Nehemiah 8:10.

Thank you, Lord, for continuous internal and external peace that passeth all understanding – Phil. 4:7.

Thank you, Lord, for making us the head and not the tail, above only and never beneath – Deut. 28:13.

Thank you, Lord, for being our shepherd – Psalm 23:1.

Thank you, Lord, because goodness, mercy, love, peace, joy, and prosperity is our portion all the days of our life – Psalm 23:6.

Thank you, Lord, for always speaking to us to direct, guide, and lead us in all we do – Psalm 32:8.

Thank you, Lord, for riches, honor, and prosperity

Thank you, Lord, for establishing and blessing the work of our hands – Psalm 90:17.

Thank you, Lord, for miracles upon miracles happening in our lives.

Thank you, Lord, for compassing us with your favor as with a shield – Psalm 5:12.

Thank you, Lord, for granting us good speed for promotions, and great testimonies that abound for us – Genesis 24:12; Luke 21:13.

Thank you, Lord, for breakthroughs and for setting open doors before us which no man can shut – Rev. 3:8.

Thank you, Lord, for perfecting all that concerns us – Psalm 138:8.

Thank you, Lord, because our path is as the shining light that shines more and more unto the perfect day – Proverbs 4:18.

Thank you, Lord, because we have arisen, and shining, and the glory of the Lord is risen upon us – Isaiah 60:1.

Thank you, Lord, for making us an eternal excellency, and a joy of many generations – Isaiah 60:15.

Thank you, Lord because all things are always working together for our good – Romans 8:28.

Psalm 92:1

> *It is a good thing to give thanks unto the LORD, and to sing praises unto thy name, O most High:*

Isaiah 43:19

> *Behold, I will do a new thing; now it shall spring forth; shall ye not know it? I will even make a way in the wilderness, and rivers in the desert.*

3 John 1:2

> *Beloved, I wish above all things that thou mayest prosper and be in health, even as thy soul prospereth.*

Thank you, Lord, for excellent health.

Thank you, Lord, for long life and prosperity.

Thank you, Lord, for making us billionaires.

Thank you, Lord, for a renewed sound mind.

Thank you, Lord, for healing all our sicknesses and diseases, known and unknown to us.

Thank you, Lord, for healing us from all bad habits and character.

Thank you, Lord, for the brand-new organs you've given to us.

Thank you, Lord, for brand-new brain, heart, lungs, kidneys, liver, and intestines.

Thank you, Lord, for brand-new genitals and reproductive organs.

Thank you, Lord, for brand-new hands and fingers, legs and toes.

Thank you, Lord, for brand-new eyes, ears, tongue, teeth, and throat.

Thank you, Lord, for brand-new arteries, veins, and capillaries.

Thank you, Lord, for brand-new bones and marrows, tissues and cells.

Thank you, Lord, for a brand-new spirit, soul, and body.

Thank you, Lord, because we are brand-new creatures, old things have passed away, and all things have become new in our lives – 2 Corinthians 5:17.

Thank you Lord, for brand-new things you're doing in our lives, making a way where there seems to be no way, making a way in the wilderness, and rivers in the deserts for us – Isaiah 43:19.

Thank you, Lord, because we will not die but live to declare your works on earth – Psalm 118:17.

Thank you, Lord, because with long life you will satisfy us and also show us your salvation – Psalm 91:16.

Thank you, Lord, because our path will always shine more and more unto the perfect day – Proverbs 4:18.

Thank you, Lord, because you are our shield, our glory, and the lifter of our head – Psalm 3:3.

Thank you, Lord, because as the mountains are round about Jerusalem, so you surround us henceforth and forever – Psalm 125:2.

Thank you, Lord, because we dwell in the secret place of the Most High God, the enemy can never see us – Psalm 91:1.

Thank you, Lord, because you are indeed our refuge and fortress at all times – Psalm 91:2.

Thank you, Lord, because we are always under your wings and feathers being shielded from all evil – Psalm 91:4.

Thank you, Lord, because henceforth no man shall trouble us because we bear in our bodies the marks of our Lord Jesus Christ – Galatians 6:17.

Thank you, Lord, because we always overcome the devil by the blood of the Lamb, and the word of our testimony – Rev. 12:11.

Thank you, Lord, for making laughter, dancing, celebrations, and testimonies our portion forever.

Thank you, Lord, for more grace and anointing to thank, praise, and worship you at all times.

Thank you, Jesus

When they finished their scriptural thanksgiving declarations unto God, they started saying "*Thank you, Jesus.*" They said it 1000 times. This is their sweet-smelling offering unto the Lord. Shaun took up his saxophone and started blowing it very passionately unto the Lord, "*Thank you, Jesus.*" As he played this unique instrument wholeheartedly and so intensely, the whole atmosphere in their suite was filled with the Spirit of God. Glorious! As he continued to play the saxophone so intensely, his wife, Mary, was slain under the anointing of the Holy Spirit and she fell down. The power of God is present in this place, touching Mary.

After about 3 minutes, she got up and screamed out aloud, "I love you Jesus. Thank you for filling me up to overflow with more anointing and the power of the Holy Spirit. Thank you, Jesus." Acts 10:38 scripture registered in her spirit so strong, and clearly. God has just visited Mary and anointed her with the Holy Ghost and with power to start doing more supernatural exploits for the Kingdom of God. Awesome!

SOME BENEFITS OF THANKSGIVING, PRAISE, AND WORSHIP

Thanksgiving brings about multiplication

Jeremiah 30:19

> *And out of them shall proceed thanksgiving and the voice of them that make merry: and I will multiply them, and they shall not be few; I will also glorify them, and they shall not be small.*

The above scripture clearly tells us that thanksgiving brings about multiplication. Therefore, thank, praise, and worship God and experience supernatural positive increases.

Jesus feeds the 5,000

John 6:9-11

> *⁹ There is a lad here, which hath <u>five barley loaves, and two small fishes</u>: but what are they among so many?*

> *¹⁰ And Jesus said, Make the men sit down. Now there was much grass in the place. So the <u>men</u> sat down, in number <u>about five thousand</u>.*

> [11] *And Jesus took the loaves; and <u>when he had given thanks</u>, he distributed to the disciples, and the disciples to them that were set down; and likewise of the fishes as much as they would.* (Underline mine)

The above scriptural passage is an account of our Lord Jesus manifesting the supernatural through thanksgiving (Verse 11) for the miracle of multiplication of 5 loaves, and 2 fishes to happen. I declare that as we give thanks, we shall also experience supernatural multiplication of every good thing we have including money in our bank accounts in Jesus' name.

Thanksgiving, praise, and worship will make a prophet speak

When a minstrel played for Prophet Elisha in 2 kings 3:15, he was inspired to speak the word of the Lord. See verses 16-20.

Thanksgiving, praise, and worship will bring down the wall of Jericho

Joshua: In Joshua 6:5-6, all Israel and the priests did was to blow the trumpets, ram's horn, sing and shout, and go around Jericho 7 days, and 7 times, and the fortified walls crumbled.

I prophesy that anything that represents the wall of Jericho in your life, like barrenness, unemployment, sickness, disease, poverty, or whatever will crumble and be destroyed today as you thank, praise, and worship the Lord in Jesus' name.

Joshua captured Jericho without raising a finger to fight. The same will happen for you. The Lord shall fight for you, and you shall hold your peace. See Exodus 14:14.

Thanksgiving, praise, and worship will defeat the enemies

Jehoshaphat: In 2 Chronicles 20:22-30, King Jehoshaphat of Judah got victory over Ammon, Moab, and Mount Seir just by Judah singing and praising the Lord. God set an ambush against the enemies, and they smote one another until everyone died, and Judah spoiled them by taking away all the abundance of their riches.

I prophesy that as you thank, praise, and worship the Lord today, He will also ambush your enemies and cause them to fight one another until they all die, and you will take away all their riches in Jesus' name.

Gideon: In Judges 7, Gideon prepared 32,000 men to fight the Midianites, but God said they were too many. The men were screened until only 300 of them were left. In Judges 7:8, these 300 men took up their trumpets and blew, and they secured their victory. This further confirms that thanksgiving, praise, and worship is a good warfare strategy.

Some examples of people who gave their substance as offering, or sacrifice to thank, praise, and worship God

God is a giver

John 3:16

> *For God so loved the world, that he gave his only begotten Son, that whosoever believeth in him should not perish, but have everlasting life.*

No one can beat God in giving. He gave His only-begotten Son, Jesus Christ, to die as a substitute for our sins. That's the highest demonstration of love. Heavenly Father, we thank you for all your love and compassion towards humanity.

Sacrifice

Psalm 50:5

> *Gather my saints together unto me; those that have made a covenant with me by sacrifice.*

When we do sacrifice unto the Lord, it touches Him, and it can be turned into a covenant with the Lord. Give your all to God, and watch Him bless you tremendously.

High Priests: They are ordained to offer gifts, and sacrifices for sins. See Hebrews 5:1 and 8:3. They also offer burnt, meat, and peace offerings and prayers unto the Lord.

Abel: In Genesis 4:4, Abel offered the firstlings of his flock unto the Lord, and the Lord had respect unto Abel and his offering. Give God your best.

Abraham: In Genesis 22, God tempted Abraham and asked him to offer his son Isaac, whom he loved, as a burnt offering on Mount Moriah, and Abraham passed the test. How? God saw that he actually had the *inten*tion to do it. See verse 12.

King David: King David said he will not offer burnt offerings unto God that will cost him nothing. See 2 Samuel 24:24-25. He offered burnt and peace offering sacrifice unto the Lord and the plague ceased in Israel.

King Solomon: He offered unto God a thousand burnt offerings sacrifice in 1 kings 3:3-5. He repeated this act and gave a much bigger sacrifice unto the Lord in 2 kings 8:63.

The King of Moab: When he saw that the battle was fierce against Israel, he offered his son that should have reigned in his stead as a burnt offering upon the wall, and Israel departed. See 2 Kings 3:27.

The poor widow: In Mark 12:41-44, this woman gave her all, which was two mites, into the treasury, and Jesus noticed her giving. Honor God with your all, and He will also notice you.

Mary: She anointed Jesus with an ointment of spikenard, very costly and precious. See John 12:3.

Disrespectful offerings to God

It is important that we don't disrespect God by giving Him peanuts, and nasty, unworthy offerings and sacrifices. As a couple, honor God with His tithes, and quality offerings and sacrifices. God spoke to the *priests* in:

Malachi 1:8

> *And if ye offer the blind for sacrifice, is it not evil? and if ye offer the lame and sick, is it not evil? offer it now unto thy governor; will he be pleased with thee, or accept thy person? saith the LORD of hosts.*

Cain: In Genesis 4:5, Cain brought to God unworthy fruits from the harvest of his farm produce to the Lord as offering, but God did not have respect for him and his offering, and he was angry. Terrible man. Don't give God or men bad gifts.

Ungratefulness – Where are the rest 9?

One of the things we must avoid in life is the attitude of ungratefulness. When you receive a gift from God or man, say, "Thank you" because that will lead to a multiplication as we have seen earlier. In Luke 17:11-19, Jesus healed 10 Lepers, but only one came back to say "Thank you" and Jesus asked in verse 17, "… *Where are the nine?*" They had disappeared. They are ungrateful.

The Bible recorded that the one that came back to say thank you was a Samaritan. And he was made *whole*. See verse 19. The lesson to be learnt here is that when we say thank you, we get more. Don't be ungrateful. Say thank you to God and men.

Beware of false worship

We must determine to worship God with a pure loving heart. If you say things you don't mean to God, that's dishonorable. The Bible says in:

Mark 7:6

> *He answered and said unto them, Well hath Esaias prophesied of you hypocrites, as it is written, This people honoureth me with their lips, but their heart is far from me.*

In the above scripture, Jesus called those who honor Him with their lips, but their hearts are from Him hypocrites. They are deceivers. Beware of false worship. Read what the soldiers did to Jesus in:

Mark 15:19

> *And they smote him on the head with a reed, and did spit upon him, and bowing their knees worshipped him.*

The above verse says the soldiers smote Jesus on the head with a reed, and spat on Him, and then worshiped Him. That's mockery and false worship, because you don't smite and spit on a person you truly worship.

How do you worship God? Do you complain about everything and then claim to worship Him? To complain or worry and worship is false worship.

God rejects sacrifices

God hates despicable sacrifices and false worship. The Bible says in:

Amos 5:21-23

> 21 *I hate, I despise your feast days, and I will not smell in your solemn assemblies.*

22 *Though ye offer me burnt offerings and your meat offerings, I will not accept them: neither will I regard the peace offerings of your fat beasts.*

23 *Take thou away from me the noise of thy songs; for I will not hear the melody of thy viols.*

Worship God in spirit and in truth

John 4:24

God is a Spirit: and they that worship him must worship him in spirit and in truth.

We are to worship God in spirit and in truth. No lies, gimmicks, or hypocrisy. Cultivate a lifestyle of thanksgiving, praise, and worship in marriage

When a couple constantly thank, praise, and worship God, this will help promote peace, and prosperity, and also keep the marriage healthy and strong.

Shaun played his saxophone again, while she sang the psalms, clapped and danced. They decided to end their very intense morning devotion.

They both got into the bathroom, cleaned up and had a bath in their Jacuzzi. When they finished, they dressed up, and sat down on the sitting room sofa, relaxing.

Today is Friday, and not normally their fasting day. However, they decided to fast today. So they are not going to the restaurant to eat. They are enjoying their thanksgiving, praise and worship, and they want to continue. They decided to rest for a while. They put on *Michael W. Smith* gospel music playlist starting with the track *Here I Am To Worship*.

After sleeping and resting, they woke up refreshed, and commenced again their intense thanksgiving, praise, and worship.

Mary continued to sing the psalms, hymns, and gospel songs while Shaun blew the saxophone.

They focussed on singing, praising, and worshiping God with:

Psalm 8:9

> *O LORD our Lord, how excellent is thy name in all the earth!*

And the hymn:

> *How Great Thou Art* by *Carl Gustav Boberg* written 1885.

Shaun played the saxophone repeatedly while she sang repeatedly.

It's now 7 pm, and time for their "*Husband and wife meeting,*" which is 7-8 pm. They both said they don't want to discuss anything today. They would rather continue with their thanksgiving, praise, and worship. They are so engrossed in the praise and worship, and they want to carry on and wish it will continue forever.

They remained indoors all day today and continued their thanksgiving, praise, and worship till 10 pm, when they finally decided to stop and sleep. They changed into their nightwear, and got into their bedroom, and under the quilt, said goodnight to each other, kissed, and slept.

CHAPTER FOURTEEN

DAY 14 – SATURDAY
IMPROMPTU CRUSADE

They woke up feeling very good and strong. They exchanged "Good morning greetings" and got into the bathroom and washed their teeth and tongues and came together in the sitting room with their Bibles and notebooks to do their morning devotion as is their custom. Then Shaun said, "Before we do today's morning devotion, I've got something very important to share with you."

Mary adjusted herself on the upholstered sofa and looking directly into her husband's eyes, she said, "Honey, I hope it's not something bad."

Shaun replied, "Oh! Not at all. As a matter of fact, it's something great sweetheart."

She said, "What is it then, darling?"

Shaun cleared his throat and said, "I had a dream in the night and God revealed to me that He has filled you up to overflow with the Holy Ghost and with power to start doing supernatural exploits for the kingdom of God. He told me clearly to support you in everything, and He said we should start immediately on a full-scale evangelical ministry work. And then I woke up." Mary became emotional with tears of joy flowing down her beautiful face.

Mary held her husband and said, "My lord and my king, I am so glad God revealed this dream directly to you. You know I told you on Sunday, New Year's Day, that I have had 3 dreams so far about this divine calling. You remember yesterday when you were blowing the saxophone so intensely during our worship, I fell down at a point in time. God visited me that time and infused me with the Holy Ghost and with power. God has gone ahead of us to give us directions, guidance, and leading regarding this evangelical work He wants us to do and I am grateful."

Shaun now said, "As soon as we get back to London, we will start taking actions regarding the dreams. Thank you, Jesus, for your love and revelations."

Shaun grabbed his saxophone and they continued their thanksgiving, praise, and worship. They are due to vacate their suite by 12 pm. They decided they have to clear up things and get ready before 10 am so that they can have their breakfast and checkout.

They finished their morning devotion, packed their things making sure nothing was left. They had their shower, dressed up and made their way to the Perfecto 5-star hotel reception to check out. As soon as they got to the reception, the Holy Spirit and the power of God started touching people so much that nearly everyone in the reception room was slain under the anointing and fell on the floor. Other people in the other parts of the hotel started looking and coming to the reception to know what was happening. As this was happening, instant miracles also began to happen. More and more people started trooping into the reception area so much that it soon filled up.

An angel of the Lord stood beside Mary as she started preaching saying, "Jesus loves you. He is here to heal you, and help you. Come and receive salvation. Today, and now is your time and day of salvation. You can't miss this glorious opportunity." The Bible says in:

2 Corinthians 6:2

(For he saith, I have heard thee in a time accepted, and in the day of salvation have I succoured thee: behold, now is the accepted time; behold, now is the day of salvation.)

As she said this, a crippled woman got up from her wheelchair totally made whole. Miracle! Another woman with a withered hand stood close to Mary and touched her, and the hand stretched forth out. Everyone started rejoicing, and thanking God. Those who were slain on the floor under the anointing of the Holy Spirit got up. Everyone started shouting out aloud.

Shaun brought out his saxophone and started playing:

Psalm 8:9

O LORD our Lord, how excellent is thy name in all the earth!

And the hymn:

How Great Thou Art by *Carl Gustav Boberg* written 1885.

Mary started singing, clapping, and dancing while others joined in. The manager saw that the reception area was now full. They opened the Hotel Auditorium, which can take up to 1,000 people. Shaun blew the saxophone with more intensity, and everyone started singing and dancing with all their might even as David danced. This is the Holy Ghost revival in operation.

The news of the miracles God is doing quickly went round the capital town, Fira, Santorini and beyond via social media, the internet, and mobile phone calls. Almost everyone in the Perfecto 5-star hotel went into the Auditorium. And within a short time, the Auditorium was now filled to maximum capacity and overflowing. Amazing! This is an unplanned crusade in action, and the way things are happening surely shows it is supernatural and divine orchestration.

A man had gone to Santorini hospital to tell them that a powerful evangelist is in Fira town with her husband. They brought many sick patients from the hospital. All the sick patients brought from the Santorini hospital were healed instantly. As Mary ministered, blind eyes opened, the dumb and deaf were healed, the lame started walking, and evil spirits started crying out of people, and people with all manner of sicknesses and diseases were healed instantly. Hallelujah!

A lot of people started struggling to touch the Woman of God, Evangelist Mary McGregor. The woman with the issue of blood for 12 years touched Jesus, and she was instantly healed. These people also believe that as they touch God's servant, Evangelist Mary McGregor, they will receive their healing. Thank God for the Perfecto 5-star hotel security staff who were on the ground to do this impromptu crowd control. As many that turned up at this unplanned crusade were made whole. Praise God!

Mary started preaching Jesus Christ to the crowd, sharing the following scriptures:

As Evangelist Mary McGregor mounted the podium of the Auditorium to preach, a Greek woman interpreter God had already prepared, also stood beside her to interpret from English to Greek for the people. The microphones the hotel uses for events were given to them.

John 3:16

> *For God so loved the world, that he gave his only begotten Son, that whosoever believeth in him should not perish, but have everlasting life.*

John 3:1-5

> *¹ There was a man of the Pharisees, named Nicodemus, a ruler of the Jews:*
>
> *² The same came to Jesus by night, and said unto him, Rabbi, we know that thou art a teacher come from God: for no man can do these miracles that thou doest, except God be with him.*
>
> *³ Jesus answered and said unto him, Verily, verily, I say unto thee, Except a man be born again, he cannot see the kingdom of God.*

4 *Nicodemus saith unto him, How can a man be born when he is old? can he enter the second time into his mother's womb, and be born?*

5 *Jesus answered, Verily, verily, I say unto thee, Except a man be born of water and of the Spirit, he cannot enter into the kingdom of God.*

John 14:6

Jesus saith unto him, I am the way, the truth, and the life: no man cometh unto the Father, but by me.

John 15:5

I am the vine, ye are the branches: He that abideth in me, and I in him, the same bringeth forth much fruit: for without me ye can do nothing.

Mark 8:36

For what shall it profit a man, if he shall gain the whole world, and lose his own soul?

Romans 10:9-10

9. That if thou shalt confess with thy mouth the Lord Jesus, and shalt believe in thine heart that God hath raised him from the dead, thou shalt be saved.

10. For with the heart man believeth unto righteousness; and with the mouth confession is made unto salvation.

Romans 10:13

For whosoever shall call upon the name of the Lord shall be saved.

Evangelist Mary delivered a powerful sermon and used the above scriptures. When she finished preaching, she made an altar call for people to give their lives to Jesus. More than 400 people showed up in front of the podium. Great! When people experience and see miracles, healings, and the power of God, they are very ready to receive salvation, and they have seen and received signs, wonders, healings, and miracles. Praise God!

She led the people to say the salvation prayer and declared them born-again Christians in Jesus' name. She advised all of them to start seeking God wholeheartedly because the Christian journey has just started. And to do this, she encouraged them to join a Bible-believing church in Fira where they also have to be dedicated members. He also encouraged them to buy a good study Bible and start studying the word of God. He also advised them to ask the leader of their church to do water baptism for them, and get them to be filled with the Holy Spirit. They must also abstain from evil, sin, and worldly lifestyles.

Prophetic word

Evangelist Mary McGregor gave a prophetic word saying, "There is a woman in this crusade. You've had 6 miscarriages, and you are currently pregnant for the 7th time. The Lord said, 'I should tell you to be strong and of good courage, and that you shall surely give birth to this baby, and the baby is destined to be great.' The woman I am talking about has a boutique for ladies. Where is the woman?" Immediately, a woman cried out aloud and raised her hands and said, "Woman of God, I am here."

Evangelist Mary stretched her hand in her direction and said, "Receive the anointing of the Holy Spirit to perfect all that concerns you and the baby in the womb."

The woman shouted, "I receive in Jesus' name." Straightaway, the power of God came upon her, and she lay on the floor being supported by two women, and a few other people also fell to the ground.

Testimonies

Evangelist Mary asked, "Does anyone have testimony?" Over a hundred people put up their hands. She now asked for three people to come to the podium to testify because of time.

First testimony

A woman came up and said, "I want to thank God for the healing miracle I received today. I was born a cripple. I was in my wheelchair at the reception when you came in and the awesome power of God hit me and my leg bones started making some crackling noise as my legs started straightening up and I immediately got up on my feet for the first time in my life today. I am so grateful. Thank you, Jesus. Thank you woman of God."

Mary asked, "How many of you here know this woman to be a cripple and in a wheelchair?" Many people raised their hands. Mary continued, "That means her testimony is true. I had to ask to clarify to anyone who is doubting the testimony. We give God all the glory for the testimony. Woman, your testimony is permanent in Jesus' name."

Second testimony

Another woman also testified thus, "I was also in the hotel when I heard that miracles were happening in the reception room. So I ran into the reception room, and as soon as I touched you, my lost left arm stretched out. I lost my left arm in a road accident 10 years ago. My left arm is now completely restored. Miracle!

Thank you, Jesus. Woman of God, thank you." Evangelist Mary replied, "We thank God for the miracle. All the glory goes to God."

Third testimony

A man was the third person, and he said, "I was a patient at the Santorini hospital. As I scrolled through my Facebook page, I started seeing messages repeatedly within minutes that healing and miracles were happening at Perfecto 5-star hotel. Immediately, a man also came into the hospital and confirmed it, and said he was at the hospital to take his mother to the crusade. So I joined them. As soon as I came into this auditorium, my very big goiter disappeared. Praise God. Thank you, Jesus. Thank you, Woman of God." Evangelist Mary replied, "We give God all the glory for all the miracles."

After the testimonies, Mary spoke with her husband, and they agreed that the meeting should be brought to a close. Evangelist Mary McGregor now made a powerful prayer and scriptural declarations for the people and the meeting ended. Glory!

The Bible says in:

*Acts 8:5-8 - **Paraphrasing***

> [5] *Then Mary went down to the city of Fira, Santorini, and preached Christ unto them.*

> [6] *And the people with one accord gave heed unto those things which Mary spake, hearing and seeing the miracles which she did.*

> [7] *For unclean spirits, crying with loud voice, came out of many that were possessed with them: and many taken with palsies, and that were lame, were healed.*

> [8] *And there was great joy in that city.*

The above scripture was fulfilled in the life of God's servant, Evangelist Mary McGregor as she preached in Fira, Santorini.

This is awesome! It's now exactly 4 pm and that means they have ministered from 10 am to 4 pm which is 6 hours in an unplanned crusade to over 1,000 people. Yet it turned out to be a huge success. Over 400 people gave their lives to Jesus, and many people received their healing. Praise God! Glory be to God!

They have not eaten since Thursday evening, and they are hungry now. They left the Auditorium and went straight to the restaurant to eat. They had missed their 2 pm earlier scheduled return flight. This means they have to book another flight ticket back to London.

Shaun is a millionaire, so the flight ticket fare is not a problem at all. These are the kind of price Ministers of God pay to fulfill God's calling. Mr and Mrs McGregor are particularly happy and satisfied that they have started fulfilling God's purpose and will for their lives.

As they got to the restaurant, they met the Perfecto 5-star hotel manager and thanked him for allowing them to use the Auditorium. The manager said they shouldn't mention it. Thank God something is free.

Shaun logged onto the internet online and saw the next available flight back to London Gatwick Airport scheduled to take off from Santorini 8 pm. He booked the flight. They served their meal from the buffet, and some drinks. They ate the delicious meal and were really satisfied.

Shaun asked her, "How do you see the impromptu crusade?"

Mary replied, "Absolutely divine and fantastic. God did this crusade so that we will know He will do whatever He wants to do, when, how, where, and with who. I am full to overflow with the joy of the Lord. We thank God for the healings, miracles, testimonies, and new converts."

They finally checked out of the Perfecto 5-star hotel. Aristarchos drove them to the Santorini airport and they boarded their flight back to London.

Four weeks after their return to London, Mary missed her menstrual cycle, and they had a bouncing baby boy exactly nine months after their memorable honeymoon. After the birth of their baby, they checked his penis, and to the glory of God, the baby's penis was perfectly normal. They named him David. King David is Mary's favorite character in the Bible. They have joy, and their joy is indeed full and overflowing. They are both radiant and flourishing with amazing grace in abundance, full of love, peace, and joy in this blissful marriage.

Mr and Mrs McGregor had just a two-week honeymoon. However, the scripture says a man should take one full year off cheering up his new wife on a honeymoon. The Bible states in:

Deuteronomy 24:5

When a man hath taken a new wife, he shall not go out to war, neither shall he be charged with any business: but he shall be free at home one year, and shall cheer up his wife which he hath taken.

King Solomon takes it further by stating that honeymoon should be every day forever for a couple. This is how he put it in:

Ecclesiastics 9:9

Live joyfully with the wife whom thou lovest all the days of the life of thy vanity, which he hath given thee under the sun, all the days of thy vanity: for that is thy portion in this life, and in thy labour which thou takest under the sun.

To live joyfully with your lovely wife all the days of your life implies every day honeymoon forever. Enjoy your honeymoon every day forever in Jesus' name. Amen!

SPREAD THE GOOD NEWS

Well done! You have successfully finished reading this book. I believe you must have picked up some principles that will help you grow in the Word of God, and spiritually as you apply them in your life. It is the application of the principles you have learnt that will bring about a transformation in your life and also give you your desired results. So, keep on practicing what you have learnt.

Now that you have read this book, and you are blessed, I would like you to tell your family, friends, and colleagues about it and spread the good news of the principles you have learnt. Recommend this book to at least twenty people you know. You can even get some copies for your loved ones as a gift. As you do this, you become a blessing to others and also enlighten the world from where you are. Thank you and God bless you abundantly.

MICHAEL NWADUBA

BIBLIOGRAPHY

1. The Holy Bible contains the Old and New Testaments. Authorized King James Version. Reference Edition. Thomas Nelson Bibles, A Division of Thomas Nelson Inc. Copyright 1989 Thomas Nelson Inc. Printed in the United States of America.
2. The Living Bible. Parents Resource Bible. A Life Application Bible. Edysyl Publications. Parents Resource Bible. Copyright 1995 by Tyndale House Publishers.
3. The Amplified Bible. Copyright 1954, 1958, 1962, 1964, 1965, 1987, by The Lockman Foundation.
4. The Thompson Chain-Reference Study Bible. Second Improved Edition. New International Version. Copyright 1973, 1978, 1984 by International Bible Society.

NOTES

1. Travel Snippet: Other Greek Islands near the Island of Santorini – https://www.travelsnippet.com/europe/greece/greek-islands-to-visit-from-santorini/ (Accessed June 25, 2025)

2. The best honeymoon hotels in Santorini – https://www.wanderlustchloe.com/best-honeymoon-hotels-santorini/ (Accessed May 29, 2025)

3. Cleveland Clinic: Male reproductive system – https://my.clevelandclinic.org/health/body/9117-male-reproductive-system (Accessed June 22, 2025)

4. Cleveland Clinic: Female reproductive system – https://my.clevelandclinic.org/health/articles/9118-female-reproductive-system (Accessed June 22, 2025)

5. Verywell Health – https://www.verywellhealth.com/average-penis-size-5087604 (Accessed May 15, 2025)

6. Sexualdiversity.org – https://www.sexualdiversity.org/sexuality/976.php (Accessed May 15, 2025)

7. OnlineDoctor.LloydsPharmacy.com – https://onlinedoctor.lloydspharmacy.com/uk/mens-health-advice/whats-average-penis-size (Accessed May 25, 2025)

8. Medical Science studies on fasting – https://www.bing.com/search?q=medical%20science%20studies%20on%20fasting&qs=n&form=QBRE&

sp=1&lq=0&pq=medical%20science%20 studies%20on%20fasting&sc=12-34&sk=&cvid= 68D9DFD21123458C8E50F603C71F263B (Accessed May 15, 2025)

9. The Museum of Prehistoric Thera, in Fira, Island of Santorini, Greece – https://en.wikipedia.org/ wiki/Museum_of_Prehistoric_Thera (Accessed May 20, 2025)

10. The Museum of Prehistoric Thera, in Fira, Island of Santorini, Greece – https://santorinidave.com/ santorini-prehistoric-museum (Accessed May 20, 2025)

11. St. John the Baptist Cathedral, Fira, Santorini – https://en.wikipedia.org/wiki/St._John_the_ Baptist_ Cathedral,_Santorini (Accessed May 25, 2025)

12. St. John the Baptist Cathedral, Fira, Santorini – https://santorini-more.com/cathedral-of-st-john- the-baptist/?v=9b7d173b068d (Accessed May 25, 2025)

13. Special Greek Food – https://www.bing.com/ search?qs=SC&pq=special+greece+& sk=CSYN1SC2&sc=16-15&pglt=41&q= special+greek+food&cvid= f2b1be840ebf4c398a6 3e079c821daf3&gs_lcrp=EgRlZGdlKgYIAx AAGEAyBggAEEUYOTIGCAEQABhAMg YIAhAAGEAyBggDEAAYQDIGCAQQAB hAMgYIBRAAGEAyBggGEAAYQDIGCAc QABhAMg YICBAAGEDSAQkxNDc3MWowaj GoAgCwAgA&FORM= ANNTA1&PC=DCTS (Accessed May 25, 2025)

14. Santorini White wines – Assyrtiko, Athiri, and Aidani – https://www.bing.com/search?pglt=41&q =Santorini+white+wines+-+ Assyrtiko%2C+Athiri %2C+and+Aidani&cvid= 33c4a1a0d38746f5bbd dfe0962651b38&gs_lcrp=EgRlZG dlKgYIABBFGDkyBggAEEUYOdIBCTIz OTA2ajBqMagCCLACAQ&FORM= ANNTA1&PC=DCTS (Accessed May 25, 2025)

15. Greek red wines – https://www.bing.com/search? pglt=41&q=Greek+non-alcoholic+red+wines &cvid=1726cec7015a4797b54dcda879b570d0 &gs_lcrp=EgRlZGdlKgYIABBFGDkyBgg AEEUYOTIGCAEQ ABhAMgYIAhAAGEAyBgg DEAAYQDIG CAQQABhAMgYIBRAAGEDSAQ kzNTE5MGowajGoAgCwAgA&FORM= ANNTA1&PC=DCTS (Accessed May 25, 2025)

16. The Island of Naxos – https://en.wikipedia.org/ wiki/Naxos (Accessed June 25, 2025)

17. Santorini to Naxos Ferry – https://www.ferry hopper.com/en/ferry-routes/direct/santorini-to-naxos (Accessed June 20, 2025)

18. Archaeological Museum of Naxos – https://en. wikipedia.org/wiki/Archaeological_Museum_of_ Naxos (Accessed June 20, 2025)

19. Archaeological Museum of Naxos – https:// archaeologicalmuseums.gr/en/museum/5df34 af3deca5e2d79e8c19a/archaeological-museum-of-naxos (Accessed June 20, 2025)

20. Healthweb Magazine: Male orgasm https://www. healthwebmagazine.com/male-orgasm (Accessed June 20, 2025)

21. Stages of male orgasm – https://sequoia.health/articles/the-male-orgasm (Accessed June 20, 2025)

22. Barriers to male orgasm – https://leighnoren.com/human-sexuality-blog/the-3-most-common-reasons-for-male-difficulty-reaching-orgasm-and-what-to-do-about-them/ (Accessed June 20, 2025)

23. Wikihow: Female orgasm - https://www.wikihow.com/Have-an-Orgasm-(for-Women) (Accessed June 20, 2025)

24. Psychology Today: Difficulty with female orgasm https://www.psychologytoday.com/gb/blog/experim entations/201802/11-reasons-women-may-have-di fficulty-with-orgasm?msockid=085c5 06ffaf4694f3 0014208fb4f68db (Accessed June 20, 2025)

25. Scientific origin: Tips for women to reach orgasm - https://scientificorigin.com/tips-for-women-who-can not-reach-orgasm (Accessed June 20, 2025)

26. Video of walking tour of Fira streets – https://www.youtube.com/watch?v=pwR1jHGQDm8 (Accessed June 20, 2025)

All scriptural references in this book are taken from the King James Version, and are in italics, except where indicated.

FOR INFORMATION, INQUIRIES, OR BOOKINGS TO SPEAK

Please send all correspondence directly to:
Email: mikenwaduba@gmail.com

OTHER BOOKS WRITTEN
BY THE AUTHOR

1. A Simple Guide for Bible Study
2. Questions and Answers on Tithes: Covenant of Prosperity
3. Amazing Grace in Abundance
4. Mr and Mrs Evans' Honeymoon on the Island of Majorca, Spain
5. Healing Balm for the Soul
6. The Holy Spirit and Supernatural Power

To order the above books, log into: *www.Amazon.co.uk*

ABOUT THE AUTHOR

 Michael Nwaduba is a Minister of God with a calling to write and evangelize. Prior to God's calling into the ministry, he obtained qualifications in Business Administration, and Accountancy. He worked for nearly two decades as a finance officer for various establishments, including being a Church Administrator for a Pentecostal Church in London.

He teaches the truth in the Word of God with a passion. He firmly believes in the integrity of the Word of God. You will find his books interesting and easy to understand because of the simple style he adopts as an author. You will also find biblical and practical life examples in his books.

Minister Mike is also a lawyer. He obtained his LLB (Hons) Law degree from London South Bank University, London, United Kingdom. He is a member of RCCG Victory House, London, and the former Personal Assistant (PA) to Pastor Leke Sanusi, Continental Overseer, RCCG Europe, and Special Assistant to The General Overseer (SATGO).